DARK
TOMORROWS

by J. L. Bryan

With Two Bonus Shorts by

Amanda Hocking

2

Table of Contents

Foreword

Thanks for picking up this copy of *Dark Tomorrows*. This collection of stories draws on my habit of writing eclectic books that have absolutely nothing to do with each other. My novels include *Helix*, a deep-future "genetic space opera;" *Jenny Pox*, the story of a teenage girl whose touch spreads a deadly supernatural plague; and *The Haunted E-book*, a ghost story about a nineteenth century tramp printer who haunts anybody that reads a certain book he made.

At this writing, *The Haunted E-book* will be released very shortly, supported by a blog tour that includes giveaways of a Kindle or two, plus the Haunted Library ebook collection (with novels donated by dozens of authors), as well as assorted ebook and paperback giveaways along the way. (Learn more at http://jlbryanbooks.com/thehauntedebooktour.html.)

The stories in *Dark Tomorrows* represent a variety of genres. "Spectrum" tells of an alien who crash lands in modern-day Tennessee. "The Fortune-Teller's Lament" is a supernatural story about a psychic who finds that a coin-operated fortune-telling machine down the street is wrecking his life. "The Long Night" pulls together deep-future science fiction and classic horror. "The Officefrau" is an example of my twisted sense of humor.

To make things even more random and eclectic, I'm very happy to bring you "The Second Coming of Pippykins" and "Of Shoes and Doom" by Amanda Hocking. Amanda is an author friend of mine who writes fantastic stories about vampires, zombies, and (my favorite) trolls, among other cute critters. This is part of a trade. Amanda is putting an excerpt of *Jenny Pox* into her new book *Honalee*, which is the first book in the Witches of Honalee series. I'm fortunate that she also gave me these two shorts to use in *Dark Tomorrows*. Obviously, I got the better end of this particular trade, but that's because Amanda is such a nice and generous person, not because I'm wily.

I hope you enjoy this collection. Feel free to contact me through my website, http://jlbryanbooks.com. Learn more about Amanda and her books at http://amandahocking.blogspot.com.

And now, for the first story...

-J.L. Bryan
12/23/2010

The Fortune Teller's Lament

Micah was late to work. Mrs. Gafford, the forty-something lawyer's wife with the huge fake tits, was already waiting for him at the Book Cauldron. She couldn't even pretend to browse among the candles and incense, or the "magic" teas, or the silver Dungeons and Dragons-type jewelry.

"Where have you been?" Mrs. Gafford demanded. "We had a ten o'clock appointment!"

"It's only like quarter after now," Micah said. He wasn't going to tell her he'd just gotten out of bed, though his hair probably made it obvious. "No big deal."

"The customer decides when it's a big deal," said Belinda, the proprietor of the Book Cauldron. She sat on the stool behind the cash register, her girth draped in lacy black cloth, her face slathered in white funeral makeup. "You don't decide."

"Sorry, Belinda," Micah said.

"What's that?"

"I mean, Lady Isis Ravenbeak." Micah had forgotten that Belinda wanted to be addressed by her "circle name" at all times now. She'd been promoted to High Priestess of her coven, probably because the last High Priestess had been transferred to another Wal-Mart two states away. The elevation in status was a very big deal to Belinda/Lady Isis.

Micah gave Mrs. Gafford his best smile. "I'll give you an extra-deep reading today," he said. "Since I was kept you waiting. No extra charge."

"Oh, a deep reading. That does sound nice." Mrs. Gafford's eyes flicked up and down Micah's body. He was twenty years younger than her, lean in the way that came with living on coffee, Ramen, and the occasional tab of MDMA.

Her husband was a partner in Gafford & Wendt, personal injury attorneys who ran cheap local commercials late at night. He was jowly and balding.

"Come on back to the Psychic Sanctuary," Micah said.

Mrs. Gafford checked her hair in a black scrying mirror with a plastic bat perched on its edge, then followed Micah through the door.

The Psychic Sanctuary was also the Book Cauldron's back storage room, cluttered with cardboard boxes and hung with the overstock of wind chimes. He moved a stack of invoices from the folding table, then pulled out a chair for Mrs. Gafford. He lit a few of the dark-colored candles that had melted into the tabletop, and into each other, in a waxy mess.

He turned off the overhead lights, then lit a stick of incense, which he waved while circling the room and muttering under his breath. All this crap—the candles, the incense, the prayerful muttering—was just to provide some drama for the client. They liked to feel like they were getting their money's worth. He played some chanty New Age CD on the stereo.

"The room is now cleared," Micah announced. He sat across from Miss Gafford, and he poked the bottom end of the incense stick into the mass of candle wax. "Would you like the cards or your palm?"

He lay his hand palm up on the table, knowing how he she would answer.

"Oh, palm! Please." She laid her hand on his and looked him in the eye. He could feel how horny she was—it crackled off her like the heat from a wood stove—but she wasn't the type to do anything, even if she wanted him. She was the type to flirt and flirt and then go home and work it off with a vibrator. She'd done it after their last two appointments.

Micah almost wished she would sleep with him. He could probably get more money out of her that way, and the apartment rent was past due.

He rubbed the edge of her palm with his thumb.

"What would you like to know today?" he asked in a stage whisper.

"I just need to know," she asked. "Is there going to be any adventure in my future? Any excitement?"

"What kind of excitement?"

"I don't know. A man, maybe."

"Aren't you married?"

"But I'm still a woman." She smiled and raised her eyebrows.

He traced a finger along her heart line and down over her Venus mound. The palm lines were nothing to him, and neither were Tarot cards.

She was going to have a little something in the near future. Not with Micah, or with any of the young men she fantasized about. Instead, she was going to have too much bourbon eggnog and screw Barry Wendt, her husband's partner at the law firm, upstairs during the Wendt Christmas party. He was even older and uglier than her husband, and he was going to come within twenty seconds, and she would feel disgusted about it intermittently for the next few years.

"You'll have an opportunity," he said, "But it won't be the kind of thing you want. If you do it, you won't enjoy it, and you'll regret it."

Mrs. Gafford frowned.

"On the bright side," Micah added, "Your husband's going to win a big case later this year. You'll have some things you wanted."

"Like that new Jaguar?" The thought thrilled her almost as much as sex.

"Very likely."

"That sounds nice, doesn't it?"

"It does," Micah agreed.

Micah saw two more clients, and then it was two o' clock and he was hungry. His hundred dollar fee was fifty bucks after Belinda's cut. With a hundred and fifty cash in his pocket, he was thinking about ordering a big spread at Waffle House. Maybe even double hashbrowns.

He opened the front door of Book Cauldron, which was strung with dreamcatchers and pentacles. The girl on the sidewalk outside turned and blocked his way. Livvie. Her hair was streaked purple and black, and her body was a display rack for her work—piercings at her eyebrow and nose, a barbell beneath her lower lip. She wore a short, black-mesh shirt that left the dragon on her midriff exposed. Through the mesh, you could see her bra, and the hybrid lotus flower/Venus flytrap on her left breast.

"Read my mind," she said.

"That's a hundred bucks an hour."

"No discount for blowjobs?" She raised her eyebrows and sucked innocently at the tall strawberry smoothie in her hand.

"Maybe."

"Don't leave that door open," Belinda snapped. "Ruins the ambience."

"Let's go to the loading dock," Livvie said.

Livvie worked at the Rusty Skull tattoo parlor, in the same strip mall as the Book Cauldron. Between the two small shops lay a vast deserted space that had once been a supermarket. It had a large, badly cracked loading dock out back, with a roof that kept off the rain, and walls that blocked the wind. Everyone who worked in the strip mall took their smoke breaks there.

They sat on the loading dock, and Micah leaned his back against the grimy brick wall. Livvie sat in front of him, cross-legged, and held out her smoothie.

"Want a sip?" she asked.

He sipped the icy drink while she held it. SanFranSmoothie was one of the other struggling businesses in the dying shopping center. Their stuff was okay.

"Lot of clients today?" she asked.

"Three."

"I got a new one," Livvie said. "Cop. Wants a giant eagle across his back. It's gonna be so expensive." She grinned.

"What are you going to do with all that money?"

Livvie set the Smoothie aside and straddled his lap. "I'm taking you somewhere." She kissed him. Her tongue prodded into his mouth, and the stud in her tongue clinked against his teeth. Micah slid a hand under her shirt and caressed her pierced nipple.

"Where are you taking me?" he whispered.

"Right here." Livvie moved her hand down to the front of his jeans and squeezed him.

"That doesn't cost anything."

"It doesn't?" She unbuckled his belt.

"Wait," he said.

"Wait what?" She unzipped his pants and reached inside.

"Stop," he said. "We can't, right here."

"We can't?" Livvie slid back off him and leaned down. She licked him, battering him with the stud in her tongue.

"Ow! Wait." He looked around. Somebody could come out of any store, at any time--for a smoke, or to talk on their cell phone, or to take trash back to the dumpster...

"Have you ever tried this?" Livvie stuck the smoothie straw in her mouth and took a deep pull. Then she put her mouth on him again and sucked—but now her mouth was filled with freezing cold liquid.

"Oh, shit." Micah grabbed the back of her head and pushed her down.

After a few seconds, sat back, smiling.

"Wait," he said. "I'm not finished."

"You're the one who told me to stop." She jumped off the loading dock. "I'm working until nine tonight."

Livvie turned her back to him and walked away.

"See you at home," Micah said.

"You can keep the rest of the smoothie."

"You're not really psychic, though, are you?" Cara asked. She exhaled a plume of Native American Spirit into his face. The bar was crowded at eleven PM on a Thursday, and the place was much too loud. Micah hadn't even wanted to go out. When he was tired, he couldn't block out the information, all the pulses of insight into the future of any person who bumped against him. Now he was crammed against the bar, with Livvie and her friend Cara.

"No, he really is!" Livvie said.

"Then why don't you, like, win the lottery or something?" Cara asked.

"It's not like that," he said. "Maybe if I met someone who was going to win the lottery--"

"What?" Cara yelled, over the music.

"If I met someone!" Micah yelled. "Who was going to win! The lottery! Maybe then!"

"Okay," Cara said. "Relax, jeez."

"It's hard to explain," Micah said.

"So what's my fortune?" Cara asked.

Livvie pulled Cara's palm close to Micah. Micah sighed and accepted Cara's hand. He didn't bother pretending to study her palm.

"What do you want to know about?" he asked.

"Money," Cara said. "I want money. Will I get some?"

Micah closed his eyes.

Cara waited tables at an upscale steakhouse in the financial district. Her boss grabbed her ass sometimes, but she put up with it because she thought she was going to meet a rich stockbroker or somebody like that. The guys she actually dated were mostly bartenders and waiters, though, because she didn't find many bankers attractive.

She was trying to get into modeling a little, too, but she hadn't told anyone because she didn't want them making fun of her. She had given a handjob to a guy who claimed to be a talent scout for the Victoria's Secret catalog, but wasn't.

Micah pushed forward into the future, trying to find any significant financial events. Nothing was sticking out to him. He could only see a few years ahead, usually. Things got gray after that.

"Not really," Micah said. "Unless you date one of those geeky financial guys that don't turn you on."

"There will be a cute one, one day," Cara said. "A cute one who's into me."

"Not as far as I can see. Just more bartenders and wanna-be musicians."

Cara snatched her hand back. "Fuck you." She covered her eyes and pushed away through the crowd.

"Micah!" Livvie said. "Why would you say that?"

"I just see what I see."

"Do you have to be that blunt about it? Did you have to make her cry?" Livvie slid off the bar stool.

"Are you going after her?" Micah asked.

"What do you think?" Livvie snapped. "Micah, not everybody's ready to know the truth about their future." Livvie disappeared into the crowd.

"Then they should stop asking," Micah said. He ordered another drink.

The next day was Wednesday, and Micah was on time at the Book Cauldron. This wasn't because he got out of bed earlier, but because his first client wasn't until eleven-thirty.

"Still only two readings today?" he asked Belinda when he arrived. She was seated at the cash register, eating a bowl of Count Chocula.

"Yeah." She didn't look up at him.

"What about tomorrow?"

She sighed and checked the appointment book. "Nothing until Friday afternoon."

"Does it seem like things are slowing down?"

"Yeah, well, that's September for you. Do more marketing. Your little Craigslist ad isn't really raking them in."

"But I'm even losing my regulars."

Belinda shrugged.

Micah sat in the folding chair under the cheap posterboard sign that said "Psychic Readings: $100/hour, $60/half hour." When he sat there— sometimes for half the day—he felt like one more useless product in

Belinda's store.

His two appointments came and went. Michah warned a young insurance executive not to go out with her friends on Saturday night, because she was going to get in a bad car wreck and break her arm. He told a schoolteacher that the man she was dating was harmless enough, but she was going to get bored with him in a couple of months because there wasn't enough drama.

He left the store and headed home early. He'd moved into Livvie's apartment, in a building converted from a rundown motel. One of the motel rooms had become the living/kitchen area, while the adjoining room was the bedroom. The place was cheap, but cockroaches were an issue.

He sat in the moth-eaten armchair, which had come with the living room and likely had been here back when the place was still a motel. He lit a cigarette and wished he had something stronger, like whiskey or pot. Coping with bright, often unexpected flashes of the future meant you needed to find ways to put your brain to sleep. But money was tight, the bills were late, and so he couldn't do much better than a pack of Dorals. Especially with his client list shrinking.

"You've been smoking in here!" was the first thing Livvie said when she got home. "Damn it, Micah."

"Sorry."

"Ugh. Come on, Cara."

Cara followed Livvie into the apartment, looking exuberant. She pointed at Micah. "You suck!"

"What?" Micah asked.

"As a psychic." She dropped onto the old couch. "You're a good faker, though."

"Leave him alone, Cara," Livvie said.

"What are you talking about?" Micah asked.

"You said there wasn't any money in my future." Cara reached into her purse, then plopped a Ziploc full of pot on the coffee table. The bag was thick—there had to be at least an ounce in there. It looked like high-end stuff, too. "And guess what? Turns out my pervy old uncle died. Left me eighty-five thousand dollars. And his vintage porn collection."

"Oh," Micah said. "Sorry about your uncle."

"He was a prickhole." Cara flipped a pack of Joker rolling papers on the table, then began breaking up a bright green bud. Livvie kissed Micah, then dropped onto the couch beside Cara.

"That's crazy," Micah said. "You asked about money. I should have seen that coming."

"Madam Rosetta did," Cara said.

"Who?"

Cara dug into her purse and tossed what looked like a small, stiff business card toward him. It twirled in midair and landed on the carpet. Micah rolled his eyes and picked it up. The card was the color of parchment.

"I asked her if I'd be getting any money," Cara said.

Micah read the card:

MADAM ROSETTA SAYS...
Your wish will be granted today.

"What is this?" he asked.

"It's Madam Rosetta, being more psychic than you." Cara laughed.

"Who's Madam Rosetta?"

"Just the stupid fortune-teller machine outside Cirque du Filet," Livvie said. "You know, that lame restaurant by the movies?"

"Never been there," Micah said.

"I was at the movies this afternoon," Cara said. "Hit the fortune teller machine before I went in. After the movie, I get the call from Uncle Ted's lawyer. It was so perfect."

"That's not possible," Micah said. "I didn't see—"

"Didn't see the future?" Cara asked.

Micah rubbed his head.

"It's okay, Micah," Livvie said. "You can't be right about everything."

"I've always been right." Micah felt a bad headache coming on. "Unless you do something to change what I predict. This doesn't happen."

"Happens now." Cara licked and sealed the joint. "Maybe I shouldn't share with you, huh? Since I bought this with money you said I wasn't going to get?"

"Whatever," Micah said.

"She's just kidding," Livvie said. "Don't get uptight."

Cara lit her joint, then slumped back on the couch. "You know," she said, "The fortune teller machine only costs a buck. Could run you out of business." She passed it to Livvie.

"I don't think so," Micah said. "A machine can't be psychic. You have to have a..."

"What?" Cara asked.

"Mind, soul, whatever. I bet it gives that exact same answer every ten times. Just has a stack of cards."

"I know where I'm getting my fortune read from now on," Cara said. "You were way, way off."

"Fine with me," Micah said. "You weren't a paying client, anyway."

"Oh, that's right," Cara said. "You get paid to be not psychic."

Livvie, who'd been puffing on the weed, snorted and laughed, which made Cara laugh, and then both of them were laughing at him.

"Sorry." Livvie gasped. "Sorry, Micah...we're not laughing *at* you...but that was pretty funny."

"It wasn't." Micah snatched the joint from Livvie's fingers. "Let me stupid up my brain, then maybe I'll laugh."

"We should go there," Livvie said.

"Where?" Micah asked. "The movies?"

"No, friggin' Cirque du Filet," Livvie said. "The waitresses dress like acrobats and crap."

"It's too expensive," Micah said. "And stupid. You just said it was lame."

"I'll pay," Livvie said. "I got some good work this week. You can come too, Cara!"

"Forget it," Cara said. "I'm not eating circus meat."

"It's like a whole theme," Livvie said. "Didn't you like the circus when you were a kid?"

"No," Micah said. "I hate clowns."

Livvie rolled her eyes. "We're going. I've been wanting to go." She sucked down more pot. "We're so going."

They went on Saturday. It was usually Micah's busiest day at work, with at least four or five clients, but today he'd only had two. His cash shortage made going to Cirque du Filet seem like an even stupider idea, but Livvie insisted.

The inside of the restaurant had big striped sheets billowing from the ceiling, as if they'd stepped into a giant tent. Life-size figurines shapes liked tigers, elephants and bears were scattered among the tables, and a carousel was parked in the middle of the room, with dining booths built into it. Calliope music played over the speakers. The floor was covered in crushed peanuts, and a man in a striped shirt and bowtie pushed a cart of cotton candy.

"Welcome to Cirque du Filet!" yelled the girls at the hostess stand, who wore glittering acrobat's costumes and top hats. "It's the greatest steak on Earth!"

"Do you have to say that every time?" Micah asked.

"Two tonight?" one of the hostesses asked. She grabbed a pair of menus designed to look like circus posters. "Would you like to sit on the carousel?"

"Um..." Micah said.

"Definitely!" Livvie said.

"Okay! Right this way!" the hostess chirped.

Micah looked at Livvie, intending to roll his eyes, but Livvie followed the hostess across the confetti-painted floor and didn't look back. They sat in a curved booth on the outer edge of the carousel. A flat-screen TV mounted near their table showing jugglers in action.

When the waitress came, Livvie picked a Daredevil Daiquiri from the specialty drink menu. Micah ordered water.

"This is fun, don't you think?" Livvie asked. "It's nice to go out somewhere."

"Yeah, it's great." Micah looked around the restaurant. The bar was a bright red semicircle illuminated by footlights. The bartenders followed some kind of sexy clown motif, the young men shirtless except for extra-wide suspenders hooked into oversized orange pants, the women in the same outfit except for a half t-shirt under the suspenders. All of them had big, bright, curly wigs and red clown noses.

At the end of the bar, he saw his client, Mrs. Gafford, drinking from a fishbowl full of bright purple liquor festooned with paper parasols and streamers. She leaned over the bar, talking to one of the male clown-bartenders. She was rubbing the bartender's hand as she spoke, and he was smiling back at her.

"That's Mrs. Gafford," Micah said.

"Who?"

"One of my regulars. She wants a fling with a younger man, but not enough to act on it."

Livvie's drink arrived—another fishbowl, this one full of red liquid and decorated with plastic devil horns and pitchforks. She took a sip through the looping straw, then she turned and looked at Mrs. Gafford.

"She looks ready to act on it," Livvie said.

"She didn't call to schedule her appointment for Monday."

"Maybe she forgot."

"I should remind her."

"She looks busy, Micah. Let's just enjoy our dinner."

"It'll only take a second. I'm starving for business."

Micah went to the bathroom first and washed his hands, so that he could pretend to notice Mrs. Gafford on the way out. He waved at her as he stepped out of the bathroom, but she didn't notice. Her eyes were on her bartender, who was mixing one of the restaurant's ridiculous large and over-decorated drinks.

"How's it going, Mrs. Gafford?"

"Oh. Micah. Hello." She glanced at him, then resumed her drooling over the bartender. She was usually a gusher of excited babble, but she didn't seem too friendly tonight. Not to Micah, anyway.

"Are you coming by on Monday?" Micah asked.

"No, thanks." Her eyes didn't move from the bartender's clown-orange pants.

"Did I do something wrong?"

She sighed, and then finally made eye contact with him. "Your last reading was way off. You said I wouldn't meet anybody, but I did."

"Who?"

"Jimmy." She pointed at the bartender. He turned at the sound of his name, smiled at her, then went back to work decorating a big blue drink with plastic sea lions.

Micah's headache began to return, and he rubbed his right temple. He hadn't foreseen anything like this. Maybe she was only flirting with the bartender, and wasn't going to hook up with him, and so Micah's subconscious had filtered it out.

"Did you just meet him tonight?" Micah asked.

"Last night. I had dinner here with my girlfriends," she said. "While we waited for our table, we used that fortune teller machine outside. I asked the same question I asked you, but she told me this." Mrs. Gafford lifted a small, parchment-colored card from her purse. It read:

MADAM ROSETTA SAYS...

Variety is the spice of life. New spices are on the way.

"Then we came to the bar, and I met Jimmy." She licked her collagen-injected lips. "When he gets off tonight...well, so do I." She laughed and took a big slurp of her bubbling Freakshow Fizz, decorated with plastic mutant heads and floating olives designed to look like eyeballs.

"I'm glad you seem happy." Micah touched her shoulder and saw a flash of her near future—getting her brains screwed out on Jimmy's sticky kitchen counter, and then against his fridge, and then on his living room floor. "Wow. You're going to have a good time."

"I don't need a psychic to tell me that." She pulled away from Micah's hand and locked her eyes on Jimmy.

Back at the table, Livvie was eating a heaping basket of Clown Fries, which were tater tots slathered in strange red, white and orange sauces.

"Get an appointment?" she asked.

"No. She left me for Madam Rosetta."

"I think I'm getting the Monkey Burger," Livvie said.

After dinner, Livvie didn't walk to the parking lot, but into the covered courtyard where the side entrance of Cirque du Filet was located, as well as the front entrance of the movie theater, and a clothing store and a frozen-yogurt place.

"Where are you going?" Micah asked.

She stopped at the fortune teller machine, whose hand-painted-looking sign read MADAME ROSETTA. The machine itself looked like an antique china cabinet, only deeper. There was a beveled glass window at the front, but the red curtains inside it were closed.

Beneath the window, there was a slot for change and a slit for dollar bills. There was also a silver button engraved with a question mark. Below this, a brass plate engraved with instructions.

"'Insert one dollar,'" Livvie read. "'Ask question. Push button. Receive fortune.' Want to try?"

"No," Micah said. "Let's just go."

"Come on." Livvie fished a dollar from her purse.

"Livvie, don't."

"Don't what?" She fed the dollar into the machine.

"Let's go."

"What should I ask? Madame Rosetta, is it true Micah and me will love each other forever?"

"Don't ask that!" Micah said.

"It's just a stupid machine."

"I don't know." Micah rubbed his temple. "She keeps changing my predictions."

"But your prediction about us was right. We already know that." They'd met six months earlier, when Livvie came in for a reading. Micah had foreseen the two of them together for the rest of their lives, seeing much deeper into the future than he ever had. He told her what he saw. Luckily, she found it cute instead of freakish, and they'd been together since.

"This feels wrong," Micah said.

"You're getting a total complex about this thing. Hey, Madam Rosetta, answer my question!" Livvie slapped the silver question mark button.

The red curtains parted. A cheesy gypsy lady mannequin sat inside, her head wrapped in a beaded scarf, her fingers hung with gaudy costume jewelry. Her hands sat on black felt on either side of a crystal ball. A few Tarot cards were also scattered on the felt—the Magician, Death, the Devil.

The crystal ball glowed, exactly as if a light bulb had been switched on inside it. Madam Rosetta's head leaned toward it, her eyes widened, and her mouth gaped open. At the same time, her hands waved up and down, doing nothing in particular except being animated. The sound of violins and clarinets—gypsy music, Micah supposed—played out of the speaker, which was brass and had the floral, flaring shape of an old phonograph amplifier.

A parchment-colored card spat out, face-down, into a little tray on the side of the machine. Livvie reached for it, but Micah grabbed her wrist.

"Just leave it," Micah said.

"You're going crazy, man." Livvie pulled her wrist free and plucked up the card. She turned it over, and they both stared at it.

MADAM ROSETTA SAYS...

No.

Livvie's brow creased as she frowned.

"It's nothing," Micah whispered. "Don't believe her. Livvie?"

"Yeah. Sure." Livvie blinked and shook her head, as if she'd been momentarily hypnotized by the card. She dropped it in her purse. "Just a stupid machine, right? What does it know?"

Madam Rosetta raised her head, and she seemed to stare right at them with her black and white mechanical eyes. Then the music stopped, the crystal ball went dark, and the curtains closed.

Micah didn't have any clients on Monday, and only one on Tuesday.

Tuesday night, he went home to find Livvie on the couch, her knees drawn up to her chin, her glazed eyeballs watching some rhinoceros mating show on public television.

"What's up?" He sat and put his arm around her, but she was stiff and didn't budge. "Livvie?"

"Hi, Micah."

"You don't look happy."

She shrugged.

"Did something happen?" he asked.

She drummed her fingers on the ripped knees of her jeans. When she spoke, her voice was soft: "What if she was right?"

"Who?" Micah followed her glance to the coffee table, where the small card sat face-up. "Come on."

"I'm not kidding. I mean, you barely help with the bills, you know? And you're not getting any customers."

"Yeah. I've noticed."

"What are you going to do?" she asked. "What's your plan for the future?"

"You know I can't see my own future," he said. "Except the flashes I get from you." He rubbed her shoulder, but he wasn't getting any glimpses of the future from her at the moment. "I can see us together, happy, old--"

"Can you see what kind of job you have? Or where we live? Or whether your shit's together or not?"

"I can't see anything about myself, except that I'm with you."

She nodded.

"I'll figure something out," he said. "You can trust me. I love you, Livvie. Nothing matters more than that, right?"

Livvie didn't say anything. On the TV, the male rhinoceros grunted and pulled out.

Micah had two clients Wednesday, but only one on Thursday and none on Friday. He sat in front of his stupid sign in the Book Cauldron and smiled at the chubby browsers and punk high schoolers, none of whom looked like they had a hundred bucks to spare.

Livvie was right. It was time to try finding a regular job. Not that there was much work in this Rust Belt carcass of a city.

She wasn't home when he got there, and he ended up passing out on the couch, listening to a scratchy Ramones LP.

He awoke much later when the front door banged open. Livvie stumbled in drunk and laughing. She toppled a skinny purple end table, and the lamp on top of it clattered to the thin carpet.

A man's laughter followed her in, and she turned and stumbled into his arms. The guy was huge and steroid-popping muscular, with a shaved head and a goatee. He wore a black t-shirt, and he had bicep tattoos—one of the broken snake from that Don't Tread on Me flag, and the other of a biker with a blazing skull riding a motorcycle, a blatant Ghost Rider knockoff.

He lifted her up, and she squealed.

"Where's the bedroom, baby?" he asked.

"Right there." She pointed, and the man carried her to the door.

"Hey, whoa," Micah said. He rubbed his eyes. "What's happening?"

"Oops." Livvie looked at the man holding her and giggled.

"Oops," the man said, and then his drunken laughter kicked in again, too.

"Yeah." Micah pushed himself up to a sitting position. "What?"

"Mi-cahh..." Livvie sang. "I'm breaking up with you." She did an exaggerated frown with her lower lip pooching out. "Sow-ry."

"When? Now?"

"Earlier." Livvie gazed into the tattooed guy's eyes. "At the bar. You just weren't there when I said it."

"Oh," Micah said. "So..."

"Yeah," Livvie said. "I mean you can crash on the couch if you want. But Ashley and me are taking the bed."

"That's right, baby." The huge guy carried her over the threshold, but then Livvie grabbed the doorframe, stopping them.

"His name's Ashley?" Micah asked.

"Oh, wait!" Livvie kicked Ashley's behemoth thighs a couple times as she wormed free of his arms. "Micah!"

"Yeah?" Micah stood up, ready for her to stumble into his arms, hug him tight, puke, and pass out.

But she didn't.

"Remember I told you about that giant eagle tattoo?" she asked. "Look. Look at this." She tugged up the back of the man's t-shirt.

"Aw, yeah, check 'er out, man." Ashley pulled off his shirt and threw it over the armchair. Then he flexed his arms and posed as if he'd entered a bodybuilding pageant. A bald eagle spread from one shoulder to the other, its tail feathers and talons reaching almost to his butt cheeks. The feathers all turned red, white, or blue at the tips, and the eagle fired a plume of bright green gas out its beak.

"Wait," Micah said. "So he's the...what's that eagle breathing out?"

"Fuckin' chlorine gas, man," Ashley said. "Ever seen what that shit does to a battlefield full of people? Talking about World War ONE, here. The original slaughterhouse."

"It's pretty bad?" Micah asked.

"Hell yeah it's bad. Guys all--" Ashley made choking noises and stuck out his tongue while clawing at his own throat. "--and shit."

"Oh," Micah said. "So, wait. You're the cop? He's the cop?"

"I guess you saw this coming, though," Livvie said. To Ashley, she said: "Micah's a psychic."

"He's a psychic?" Ashley smirked. "Then I guess you know what's going to happen next."

"Actually, that's not how--"

Ashley picked up Livvie again, carried her to the bedroom, and threw her on the bed. Livvie took off her shirt.

"Wait!" Micah said.

"Out, dude." Ashley pointed to the front door. "Out. Or look into the future and see me, kicking your ass."

Micah grabbed his jacket and his car keys.

He drove away in his rattling old Corolla. It was almost two in the morning. He hit a grungy basement club with a crappy live band, just in time to order three shots of well tequila at last call. It cost him the last of his cash. He gulped the first one down, and then tried to figure out what to do next, after the bar closed.

Maybe tomorrow he could call Tony, but Tony's girlfriend didn't like Micah staying at his place and probably wouldn't let him move back in. He tried to think of other people to call.

He drank his second shot. His brain grappled with his new condition—single, homeless and basically unemployed.

His thoughts kept circling back to the fortune telling machine. The ridiculous old-fashioned hokeyness of it, the gypsy waving her mechanical hands and casually changing the futures he predicted. Practically granting wishes, even. All for a dollar. How could he compete with that?

After his last shot of tequila, Micah drove over the Shopping Village Plaza, home to the Cirque du Filet and the multiplex cinema. It was deserted, but the movie marquee and the neon-clown restaurant logo burned all night.

He parked and rooted in his trunk, among dirty socks and broken CD cases. He found a tire iron, then slammed the trunk lid.

Micah walked into the covered courtyard area, with its benches and potted plants, outside the business entrances. He approached the Madam Rosetta machine and stared at the red velvet curtains behind the glass pane.

"Tough life, huh?" he asked. "You know what they always say to me? 'Why don't you win the lottery?' 'Why not play the stock market?' 'Hey, you should...you should have seen this coming!'" He bashed the tire iron into the glass, and a vertical crack split the pane from top to bottom. He swung again and shattered the left half of the pane into a thousand bright pieces. Glass splinters bit into his knuckles and forearms, drawing blood, but he barely noticed.

"And you know what I tell them?" he asked. "Of course you know." He smashed out the right half of the broken pane, but he didn't get as clean a break this time. Big glass teeth still clung to the edges of the frame.

He grabbed the red velvet curtains and ripped them loose. They smelled like mildew and rat droppings. He tossed them to the concrete.

Madam Rosetta sat inside her box, staring straight ahead, black eyes open, hands resting on either side of the crystal ball.

"I tell them," he said, "It's not like that. Ever try to read numbers in a dream? Ever try to read a fucking book in a dream? It's all garbage. Something has to make an emotional mark before I can see it."

He raised the tire iron again.

"What are you?" he asked. "Why are you doing this to me?"

Madam Rosetta remained frozen.

He glanced at the silver button engraved with the question mark.

"Oh, hell," he said. "Why don't you tell me?"

He fished change from his pocket, since he was all out of paper money. He fed them into her coin slot.

"What are you?" He pressed the silver button.

The crystal ball illuminated, the gypsy's hands moved up and down, and she widened her eyes and gazed into the ball. Music played out the phonograph horn.

A card spat into the side tray.

MADAM ROSETTA SAYS...
What you seek, you will find.

"That's great. Thanks." He crumpled the card and threw it into Madam Rosetta's face. It bounced off the dark spot of blush painted on her cheek and dropped to the black felt, next to her Tarot cards. "Why do you keep changing my predictions? And how?"

He pressed the question button again. She gazed into her crystal ball and waved her hands up and down. Machinery whirred inside the cabinet.

Then the light in the ball went out, her hands lowered, and her face tilted up until she was looking at him. The music stopped, and the whirring machinery fell silent.

"Oh, guess I need to insert another dollar," he said. He raised the tire iron. "How about if I just beat it out of you?"

Madam Rosetta didn't respond.

Micah smashed her crystal ball with the tire iron. The interior was empty except for a light bulb, and he smashed that, too.

Then he swung the tire iron into her face. Her plaster nose cracked and fell away in chunks.

He struck her again, and a web of cracks spread across her face.

He hit her a third time, and the chunks of shattered plaster fell away.

Behind the face was a skull. The machinery that moved her eyes and mouth had been screwed to the skull's eye sockets and jaw. There was no reason to create such a detailed and realistic fake skull and place it where no one would see it, Micah thought. The skull looked much more real than Madam Rosetta's face had.

Blinding white lights flooded him from the direction of the parking lot.

"Stay right there," a voice commanded.

Shit, the cops, Micah thought. He dropped the tire iron, and it clanged against the concrete. Metallic echoes reverberated across the enclosed courtyard. He raised his hands, palms open, and squinted against the light.

A dark male silhouette approached him from the lights. The silhouette raised both his hands. It looked like he held a gun in each one, and was pointing them at Micah.

"I'm not armed," Micah said. "What do you want me to do?"

"Stay still."

The silhouette fired both his weapons, but with a weird downward crank using his thumbs. Long, thin chains sprang from his sleeves, each chain tipped with two iron semicircles.

These smacked into Micah's wrists, then clamped shut, cuffing him.

"What the hell was that?" Micah looked up at the iron rings around his wrists, and the long coppery chains that stretched all the way back the man's baggy jacket sleeves. And now Micah could see that the person approaching him wasn't a cop, but a very short man in a baggy woolen jacket, which had been repaired many times with patches and crude stitching. He also wore a woolen cap pulled low, almost to the top of his bushy red beard.

The gnomish man walked backward, toward the light. He seemed to be unspooling more chain, because he wasn't pulling on Micah at all. More chain fell from his sleeve and clunked on the concrete.

"What are you doing?" Micah asked. He pulled back on the limp chains. They were incredibly heavy, for being so thin.

The man walked too close to the light source for Micah to watch him any more. He heard some loud clanking ahead. Then the chains began to flow toward the light. They rose up from the concrete, drawing more and more taut.

The floodlights snapped off. The chains led up a ramp, into the back of a box truck.

"Come on, don't," Micah said. "Look, whatever you want from me, I probably don't have it, so--"

The chains snapped tight and straight, and then hauled him forward. Micah jogged to keep up with them, but they accelerated faster than he expected and pulled him flat on his face. They dragged him the last ten feet to the truck, and then up the ramp.

Inside the truck, they dragged him until he was flat against the wall of the truck, dangling from the ceiling. Above him, he could see where the chains had coiled up onto ceiling-mounted, gear-driven spools. The ceiling above him was covered in rotating gears, chains, and hissing hoses.

Two other walls were hung with tools, which looked archaic to Micah, like an iron hand drill, or a hammer with an uneven head and knotty handle, clearly not made in any modern factory. Against another wall, he saw gypsy scarves, magicians' top hats, pointy witch hats, a rack of robes. The back of the truck was half workshop, half theatrical dressing room.

A brass device rolled out from the wall. It looked like a hand truck, but with the big spoked wheel of a wheelchair. As it turned, Micah saw the small bearded man steering it.

"Hey!" Micah shouted. "Hey, dude!"

The little man ignored him and wheeled the hand truck down the ramp. Micah watched him slip the prongs of the hand truck under the fortune teller machine. He tilted the machine forward, spilling broken glass and Tarot cards onto the concrete. Then he wheeled it up into the truck and positioned it against the far wall, directly across from Micah.

"Hey," Micah said. "Is that a real skull in there?"

The man kicked a lever in the floor, and the ramp retracted from the ground and clattered away underneath the floor of the truck, as if it had been mounted on a stretched-out spring. The truck rumbled and drove away from the shopping center, and the overhead door at the back of the cargo area dropped into place.

"Where are we going?" Micah asked in the dark.

A lantern flared, and the man hung it from a dangling hook. It gave a swaying light as the truck accelerated. Micah looked toward the cab area of the truck, but it was sealed behind a solid wall hung with hand saws.

"Rosie," the man said. His voice reminded Micah of a croaking frog. "Nearly time to pack her in, anyway. The ectoplasm leaks slow, but it leaks."

"The what?"

"One hundred and forty years in operation." He took a fat ring of keys from his belt, licked his thumb as he sorted through them, then unlocked the front of the Madam Rosetta cabinet. He swung it open. "No electricity, except the light bulb. All driven by springs and weights."

The interior of the cabinet was a latticework of gears, levers, weights, and pulleys. Micah could see wire frames holding stacks of parchment-colored cards, and the rollers and chutes that fed them toward the answer tray on the side.

"She's a work of art," the little man said. "First built her in 1872. Haven't done a thing but polish the wheels, wind the springs and update her to accept paper money."

"Is that...a real person in there?" Micah asked. "What did you do?"

"You're asking? I would think you'd find it obvious by now." The man opened the cash and coin receptacle mounted inside the cabinet's front panel. He dumped the money into a cracked leather box. "She wasn't 'Madam Rosetta' in life. Or even a Romany. She was a gifted Irish lass, Shanna. She could speak with the spirits of the dead, too. Shame to waste such power on such a simple machine, when you think of it."

"Why did you do it?"

"Because I haven't got a design for a 'Speak to the Dead' machine," the man said. He began disassembling Madam Rosetta's internal gear matrix with a hand drill and screwdriver. He lowered a weathered plank of a worktable from the side of the truck and locked it into place. "Don't know if there's a market. Plus, deadspeak is a rare talent, and those with it tend to go loopy fast. So, not much of a stable supply, either. No reason to launch a new product line." He placed clockwork gears and long, thin screws on the table. The lower half of each screw was encrusted with black gunk.

"But why do this to a person at all?" Micah asked.

"Oh, I'm no philosopher. Just a mechanic, doing my job." He continued disassembling the Madam Rosetta machine, laying the parts in even rows across the work table.

"Who do you work for?" Micah asked.

"Oriax Amusements." The little man beamed. "Founded in good old Eridu. Providing wonders, spectacles and diversions for the human soul for over five thousand years. I have furnished automata for more priests, sultans and would-be god-kings than you could ever name. My contraptions delighted mobs in the Roman Forum, operated by copper coin, counterweights, and water power." His smile revealed teeth that were unnaturally sharp, most of them crooked and black. "I have put on grand displays in the temples of Babylon, the Circus Maximus, the imperial court at Constantinople."

"But you just do this now?"

The little man scowled. "Times change." He took off his woolen hat, revealing a mass of knotted, dirty red hair, as well as a pair of stumpy goat horns protruding from his forehead. He scratched his head, then replaced the cap. "Like now. They say my automata are too old-fashioned.

They want new, glitzy things, digital, holographic. And we must feed the customer what he demands, must we not?"

Micah pulled on the iron cuff around his right wrist, but it was locked tight. "You can let me go," Micah said. "I won't tell anyone what I saw."

"What you saw?" The little man studied him and sucked one of his fang-like incisors. "Ah. You think I'm afraid of getting caught by some human authority." He croaked out a laugh. "If the Achaemenid Immortals could not slay me, I don't see why I should fear your donut-eating constables."

"The who?"

After extracting all the bronze and iron machinery and laying out each piece, the little man dropped the long, gunk-encrusted screws into a tin bucket full of brown liquid, where they sizzled.

"We are down one machine," the little man said. He pulled the body of Madam Rosetta—or Shanna the Irish psychic—out through the open door in the cabinet. He stripped the scarf, wig, blouse and costume jewelry, leaving just a shriveled corpse. Shanna had been a small, short woman, or maybe just a girl. Micah felt a pang of sorrow for her.

The little man dropped her body into a burlap sack and gave it a kick. It slid away into a far corner.

"What are you going to do with her?" Micah asked.

"What do you care? You've got your own problems." The little man grabbed two more open iron rings dangling from chains. The chains uncoiled, clanking, from spools on the ceiling as the man approached Micah. The man dropped one of the rings and grabbed Micah's left foot.

"No!" Micah drew back his shoe and kicked the man in the face as hard as he could manage.

The little man shrieked as he somersaulted backward, then landed facedown on the floor of the truck. He looked up at Micah. His lower lip was split open and bleeding.

"That hurt," the man hissed. "I was trying to be nice to you. I liked your attitude. No more."

The man hopped to his feet. He flung the open iron rings at Micah, and they cracked into both of Micah's ankles. Micah hissed in pain. The rings closed tight around his ankles, squeezing the freshly bruised bone. Micah cried out.

The man turned a crank on the wall. The wooden wall slab against which Micah was chained swung out until Micah lay flat on his back, staring into the oily gears and chains arrayed on the ceiling. Then the platform lowered until he was waist-high to the little man. The little man pulled a lever on the side of the crankbox, and the platform bounced as it locked into place.

The man approached him with a smile.

"If you're going to kill me," Micah whispered. "Just make it fast."

The man lifted a straight razor with an ivory handle from his leather tool belt. He unfolded the long blade. "Is that what you want?"

Micah swallowed. He was too scared to speak, and he had no idea what to say.

The man moved closer and lay the blade across Micah's throat.

"Please," Micah whispered. "Just let me go."

"I've been watching you," the man said. "You're good enough. Nothing like Shanna was, but there's juice in you. You don't deserve her beautiful cabinet, though. I have something else in mind." The man scraped the razor up Micah's jaw. Then he repeated the movement, taking off some of Micah's skin. "I could have used soap and water, you know. If you hadn't tried that stupid attack."

"What did you expect me to do?"

"You could thank me."

"Huh?"

"You're alone. You're suicidal. You needed a new life. Along I come with a fantastic offer." The man scraped both of Micah's cheeks, then shaved off his eyebrows. He hacked at Micah's unkempt black hair.

"What offer?"

"Work," he said. "Job security. A position from which you can't be removed." He croaked another laugh.

"What if I say no?"

"You can't say no." The man worked quickly—he was scraping Micah's scalp raw now. "You already said yes when you smashed up my machine, as I measure things."

"I'll pay you money for it," Micah said. "Just let me go."

"You don't have any." The man pushed the pile of Micah's hair off the platform with a dirty rag. "And I wouldn't want it if you did. I earn my own keep."

"Please," Micah whispered.

The man held up a device that looked like a leather gas mask, with a tube that reached up to a distended sphere of bottle glass, which sat inside an antique birdcage bolted to the ceiling.

"What's that?" Micah asked.

"In case your ectoplasm slips out during the procedure." He

pressed the mask to Micah's face and pulled the strap tight. The leather smelled like vomit and blood.

The man adjusted the iron rings on Micah's wrists, slid them midway up his forearms, then locked them in place. He framed brackets around Micah's wrists. Then he lined up a long screw in a bracket hole against Micah's left wrist, and Micah felt its sharp tip poke into his skin, drawing blood.

Micah shook his head, but the man turned the screw with the hand drill. The screw pierced between the bones of Micah's wrist and drove out the other side, while Micah screamed into the mask. The man capped the screw with a washer and nut. Then he repeated it with Micah's other wrist, while Micah writhed and bucked in pain.

Micah's blood pumped out into two growing puddle on the table.

The man cut off Micah's clothes with sewing scissors. Then he mounted more brackets along his body, installing sockets at his wrists, shoulders, ribs, and knees. Micah felt himself blacking out from the pain, but he fought against it.

The little man turned a crank, lifting Micah on the chains, away from the platform. A mechanical arm holding all four spools of chain swung Micah deeper into the truck. The man folded Micah's wooden platform back against the wall and locked it in place.

The chains pulled Micah into a standing position, then lowered him into a vertical silver-colored tube, which was currently split in half to reveal the brass clockwork machinery inside. Rings of light bulbs were mounted on the outside—red, blue and yellow rings, in an alternating sequence.

He screwed Micah's knees to a frame inside the tube, and then drove more long screws between Micah's ribs. The pain overwhelmed Micah, and the world turned dark.

Micah floated up a long, dark tunnel towards a distant spot of light. The spot grew larger, and then Micah spilled out into the bottle-glass sphere. Everything in the truck looked distorted through the thick glass, as if it were all underwater. Micah tried to push against the glass, but he had no hands. He looked around for an opening through which he could escape, but the glass was solid.

Below him, he watched the man mount his body in the cylinder, and then screw a long strip of metal to Micah's spine. This kept Micah's body in an upright posture. The man threaded wires through the brackets at Micah's wrists and shoulders, then down along his spine, finally hooking them into wheels in the machinery inside the cylinder.

He screwed more mounts and wires into Micah's jaw, and then into the bone by each of his eye sockets.

Micah felt no pain, and that frightened him.

The man opened a drawer in one of his tool racks, and he brought out a pair of porcelain eyeballs that each had a tiny gear train mounted on the back.

"I had to paint these special," the man said to Micah's corpse. "For the black light. What do you think?"

Micah's corpse didn't reply.

The man slapped Micah's face. Then he looked up at the glass sphere. "Oh, there you are. Good." He screwed a nozzle in the tube shut, then took the mask from Micah's face and let it dangle loose. Then he mounted the mechanical eyeballs over Micah's eyes.

The little man dressed Micah in aluminum-colored robes with electric-blue fiber optic threads. From his costume rack, he picked out a white turban with a big green chunk of costume jewelry on the front, and a long white beard. He fitted these onto Micah's head, then looked up at the glass sphere. "What do you think?"

Micah had no voice, and no way to answer.

The man installed him one night at a video arcade in Put in Bay, Ohio, on Lake Erie. Micah had a tinted glass dome over him, so he would remain in shadow until someone fed in money. The man had constructed and painted a plaster face over his real one, dressed him in the turban, beard, and fiber-optic robe, and then painted "Dr. Futuro" in glowing paint on the front of the cylinder.

A tiny glass bulb in each of the mechanical eyes held a puff of Micah's ectoplasm, so he could look out. The impish little man plugged him in, presented the arcade manager with an invoice, and left.

The arcade closed shortly after that, and Micah spent the whole night looking at the flickering video screens of dance games and stock car simulators.

The next day, customers checked out the new Dr. Futuro machine.

A record inside the cylinder played advertisements: "Come witness the wonders of Dr. Futuro!" and "Who dares to learn their future?" The voice came out through a black mesh square that looked like a modern amplifier, but concealed behind it was an old phonograph horn.

His first customers were a couple of teenage girls wearing fanny packs, clearly tourists.

"I want to know my future!" one of them said. She fished out a dollar and fed into a slot on the front of the silver cylinder. The cylinder was like Madam Rosetta's cabinet, concealing the lower half of Micah's body, as well as all the mechanisms.

A black light switched on inside the dome. Micah's turban, eyes, beard and robes glowed in ghostly greens, as did the crystal ball mounted on the black felt—officially, the crystal ball was the "quantum reflector," another bit of marketing nonsense, and the little demon-man had even painted an atom on the front of the glowing glass ball.

Inside the cylinder, a mechanical arm changed records, and then the needle dropped again.

"I am Dr. Futuro!" the voice boomed over the speaker. "Ask your question and press the gold button!"

The two girls laughed, then whispered to each other.

After ten seconds, the record repeated: "Ask your question!"

"Okay, chill out, Doctor Futuro!" one of the girls said, and her friend laughed.

"Hey, I know," said the girl who'd fed in the dollar. "Am I going to make out with that Joey guy or not?"

She pressed the gold button.

Inside the cylinder, a circle of gold pressed against Micah's heart. A weak current flowed from the girl's fingertips to his heart, enabling him to get a slight flash from her.

His mechanical hands waved up and down around the glowing green crystal ball, while his eyes and mouth moved, and his head turned a bit from side to side. On the hidden record player, the needle lifted, then dropped into the second groove. An array of laser-beam sound effects and rapid techno music played.

She wasn't going to make out with Joey, because Joey was going to make out with her friend instead. She would be mad about it for months. Their friendship would deteriorate, especially when school started in the fall.

Micah had ten pre-recorded answers from which to choose, include three variants each of "yes" and "no."

The needle dropped into the fifth groove.

"You will not get your wish!" the voice of Dr. Futuro boomed. "The opposite will come true!"

"Pfff, whatever," the girl said. "I'm totally getting that guy."

"Yeah," her friend said. "We totally are."

They walked away.

Micah remained where he was.

The arcade grew busier over the months, as summer tourist season swelled. Dr. Futuro developed a reputation for uncanny accuracy, and a base of regular customers.

In July, he heard a familiar voice boom across the arcade. Through the crowd, he could see the big cop with the goatee, much of his bald eagle tattoo visible between the straps of his tank top. He was playing Zombie UFO, a game that involved standing on platform that tracked your movement, holding a huge plastic gun, and shooting zombie aliens on a big screen. Ashley the cop had just splattered an alien that looked like a glowing green octopus. Its tentacles wriggled in pools of blood all over the chrome floor of a space station repair bay.

"Ho-yeah!" Ashley barked.

"Are you done yet?" Livvie stood at the side of the platform with her arms folded.

"Go play ski-ball again, baby!" Ashley yelled. He was blasting his way through a morgue full of slobbering alien zombies. "I'm busy!"

"I'm sick of ski-ball. And I'm sick of pinball, too. This is a crappy way to spend our vacation."

"Then go play whack-a-mole."

"I'll play whack-a-mole on your dick." She stalked away.

"Shit, you better!" he yelled after her. This caused him to miss the little gray alien with the giant shark teeth, which ripped off his character's head.

"Game over!" his screen announced. "Insert two dollars to continue!"

Livvie wandered up to the Dr. Futuro machine. Micah watched her through the tinted glass, feeling a terrible ache at being unable to move or speak to her. Once, they'd been meant to be together, but now he could barely recall those visions.

"Dr. Futuro," Livvie said.

"Dr. Futuro knows your future!" the record announced.

"Does he?" Livvie asked. She leaned close, peering through the tinted glass at his face.

"Hey, babe, want your fortune?" Ashley pulled out a dollar.

"No. I hate these things." Livvie stepped back.

"Aw, don't be a scaredy-cat." Ashley fed a dollar into Dr. Futuro.

The black light flared, and Dr. Futuro raised his head and looked at Livvie. "Ask your question!"

"Go on, baby," Ashley said. "Ask whatever you want." He grabbed

Livvie's ass, and she smiled.

"Dr. Futuro," Livvie said, "Do Ashley and I have a happy future together?"

Livvie pushed the gold button, and Micah had a weak taste of her energy. For a moment, he could almost remember how she felt against him, how she smelled.

He sent the record needle to groove thirteen, the last and innermost groove, which held Dr. Futuro's most bombastic answer.

"That will never happen, you fool!" the recorded voice boomed, and Livvie took a step back. She glanced uncertainly at Ashley.

With all his willpower, Micah seized complete control of the record mechanism. He raised the needle, then bashed it down, scratching the record. Then he dropped the needle into the thirteenth groove again.

"Never—never—never—" the skipping record repeated. He made the black light flare until his eyes and beard seemed to burn with bright green fire. He turned his upper body directly at Livvie, his jaw moving up and down in time with the record, his hands pounding up and down on the felt. "Never—never—never—"

"Let's go," Ashley said. "That thing's creepy."

"Yeah." Livvie kept staring at Micah's burning green eyes.

"Never—never—never—" the record played.

Dr. Futuro's hand lifted high, then he smashed his own crystal ball. A jet of sparks shot up inside the dome, casting fiery red and yellow light across his face. One of his shifting-hologram "Space Tarot" cards caught fire. It was a Major Arcana card, The Black Hole.

"Come on!" Ashley grabbed Livvie's hand and hauled her away. Dr. Futuro turned to watch after them, and the volume of his voice rose, filling the entire arcade, while game system after game system crashed and turned black.

"Never—never—never—" Dr. Futuro predicted.

The Officefrau

I found myself hiding in the break room supply closet, staring out through the door vent at the refrigerator, for perfectly logical reasons.

First, understand I'm really a keep-to-myself type. I do better with machines than humans, unless those humans are communicating to me via machine. The IT department at Deuschenhoffer Doorknobs (Minneapolis) consists mostly of guys like me, pale from lifetimes parked indoors in front of glowing monitors. We're either skinny or chubby, no in-between, but we all eat the same diet: corn chips, Little Debbies, and colas caffeinated to the legal limit.

Stacy Klingerschmidt was the exception. Everybody pretended not to notice she was a tall, blond, uncomfortably attractive female, an exotic Jane Goodall among us apes. We pretended not to drool over the short hippie dresses she wore on Fridays. She was a good network admin, so it was easy to talk to her on a professional level, at least, provided you did it by email and not in person. In person, it was hard to look at her and work your mouth at the same time.

Within a month of her start date at Deuschenhoffer, Stacy began bringing me all her complaints about the job. I don't know why. I don't have any influence. I'd like to say it was because of my charm, wit, and good looks, but it wasn't. I was twenty-three and hadn't had a girlfriend since Myra Chadwick in the tenth grade, who kissed me but left me three weeks later, when Bret Kjertsen won the Twin Cities Chess-Off.

Maybe Stacy liked that I just sat there nodding my head, never losing interest in her face or voice. I just blinked and grinned like an idiot, no matter how much she rambled on and on and on—mostly about her lunch.

"My Carbless Cuisine's gone again," she might say, usually around twelve-fifteen. She'd walk into my cube and sit on my desk when she talked to me, her yoga-toned thigh dangerously close to my mouse hand.

"I can't believe they took the Turkey and Pea Pizzazz. That's the grossest one."

"I'm sorry," I'd say. Once, I suggested she get a Pop-Tart from the break room vending machine. That brought a look of disgust from her, followed by a long rant about corn syrup and bleached flour, so I stopped offering advice.

"Six days," she said on that particular Tuesday, the day before I ended up in the closet. "They took my lunch six days in a row. They're ruining my diet, Dave! I starve all day and end up binging at night, and now my butt's blimping up. Look at that."

Stacey hopped off my desk and turned her back to me. Her butt looked amazing to me, under her stretchy black slacks, but I didn't know if I should tell her that. She could file a sexual harassment claim. It was in the employee manual.

"You look...okay," I finally said."I mean I don't think you look bad." I felt stupid.

"Thanks," she said, but it was an automatic response. She looked at me with miserable, glistening eyes. "I appreciate that, but…"

I could guess the rest of her sentence: *...I'm not really trying to impress guys who probably get off just looking at a hot chick in a video game.* (Which I don't, by the way. It was just the one time in high school, and I never played *Tomb Raider* again.)

Hoping to win Stacy's heart with my courage and chivalry, I decided to hide in the break room supply closet the next day and keep watch on her lunch. I didn't mention the idea to her, in case it failed.

My supervisor happened to be out of town, and I wasn't assigned to the help desk until Thursday. Really, I don't know if anybody would have noticed if I hadn't showed up to work at all.

So I arrived early Wednesday morning and took up my post. I knelt in the supply closet, watching the break room through a slotted vent panel in the lower third of the door. I had a good bead on the fridge, and I'd already topped up the bins of creamer, sugar, stirrers and napkins on the counter, so nobody would need to open the supply closet and discover me huddled inside.

People began trickling through at about seven-thirty, stowing lunches in the fridge, pouring a cup of coffee, then either stopping to chat or hurrying out of the room. Somebody dropped off a half-full box of donuts. Somebody else, a leftover hunk of birthday cake.

I held my breath when Stacy entered. Her butt really was a little bigger. For the first time, I considered maybe she hadn't always been gorgeous. Maybe in high school, she'd been an acne-blighted porker like me. The thought filled me with hope, and a renewed sense of responsibility for her microwaveable lunch.

Stacy stashed her purple Carbless Cuisine box at the back of the freezer. She'd written her name on it in fat black marker.

She cast a suspicious glance at a pair of pudgy, balding accountants eating donuts by the coffee machine, then shifted a few other microwaveable lunches over to hide her Cuisine. She closed the freezer, then glared at an overweight administrative assistant who entered the break room as Stacy left.

After nine, the room fell silent. I tried to shift from my painful kneeling position to a hopefully-less-painful squatting position, but my legs had fallen asleep and were as weak as spaghetti noodles.

The smaller second-coffee crowd started arriving about ten, and they were all gone by ten-thirty. I remained in the closet, feeling stupid, hoping nobody had noticed I wasn't in my cube. I considered how best to regain my feet, given the numb state of my legs. I grabbed a shelf loaded with boxes of plastic spoons and began pulling myself up.

Then Gerta arrived.

At the time, I didn't yet know her name was Gerta, but I did recognize her from around the office. When there was birthday cake, she strove for a frosting-rich corner piece. When there was a holiday party, she walked along the buffet heaping food onto an overloaded paper plate, constructing a massive pyramid of potato salad and bread rolls.

Gerta was a remarkably obese woman who looked to be in her mid-fifties, with layers of chins and jowls puddled around her mouth. She favored sweaters inset with beadwork depicting kittens, bunnies, and/or teddy bears. Today, it was teddy bears. Her hair was dyed an unnatural dark red and set into a perm. She could occasionally be heard complaining about the builder's heaters, or the air conditioning, or the latest episode of *Dancing with the Stars*.

Deuschenhoffer Doorknobs was the world's third-largest doorknob manufacturer, proud to still make their products in the USA--except, of course, for the components. They had over a thousand employees in Minneapolis. At least fifty of these more or less matched Gerta's description. She was a standard office type. You could find her ilk in any department—administrative, accounting, human resources—the more bureaucratic the environment, the better they thrived.

On the cubicle farm, Gerta was just one more native species, the kind you hoped didn't sit next to you at the office picnic to regale you with the long, tortured history of her troubles with the podiatrist.

I froze in place, unsteady on my numb feet, half-squatting behind the closet door, clinging to the shelf for balance. I didn't want to make a sound.

Gerta approached the fridge. Her hands were empty, so I knew she'd be making a withdrawal, not a deposit. She glanced back at the break room door several times, then opened the freezer and rummaged through the contents.

There was definitely something shifty happening here.

Gerta looked to the door again, then back at the frozen meals, and then she puckered her lips. They stretched forward more than an inch from her face. And they kept stretching, drawing the flesh of her face out into a long hose. Her many chins and jowls unfolded and stretched taut as the tube grew longer and longer.

The tube, now two feet long, probed like an elephant's trunk among the frozen meals. It coiled around the purple Carbless Cuisine box, lifted it, tore it in half.

Her lips, at the tip of the fleshy trunk, peeled the clear film from the purple plastic dish. She sucked up the frozen puck of beefsteak, then the icy cauliflower/broccoli lump.

The frozen food slurped back through her trunk, cracking to pieces along the way, as if she had teeth or vise-like muscles in there. She swallowed them down into her vast body.

After devouring Stacy's lunch, Gerta's mouth tube pried open a box of Girl School cookies. She vacuumed up two rows of Thin Mints. I could see them travel up through the long tube to her face. It sounded like a cement mixer full of pebbles.

"--just crazy," a male voice said as the break room door opened. It was Maurice Schultz, current VP of marketing, talking to Elisha Berger, director of product development.

"A door-*knob* is one thing," Schultz was saying. "A door-*bell* is another. You don't go combining the two. It's unnatural." Maurice noticed Gerta at the fridge. "Oh, hello, uh…"

"Gerta." Gerta had transformed back to her usual self, and she was closing the freezer door with a grumpy look on her face.

"Right," Schultz said. "Of course. Gerta. Must have slipped my mind."

"Can you believe they voted off Gary?" Gerta asked.

Maurice and Elisha exchanged looks.

"What do you mean?" Elisha asked.

"On *Dancing with the Stars*. He was my favorite. Didn't you watch?"

"Sorry," Elisha said.

"It's all rigged, I'll bet ya. They just want the pretty girl to win." Gerta lumbered out of the room, shaking her head.

Maurice and Elisha fell right back into their conversation, as if Gerta hadn't left the slightest impression on either of them. I thought of a vampire hypnotizing his victims. Or the flashy thing from *Men in Black*. I watched the two executives and waited for my chance to come out of the closet.

I didn't mention it to Stacy, or anybody, the next day. There was no way to explain it. Gerta wasn't human. She was some kind of space alien, maybe. But what kind of alien intelligence crossed the galaxy to spend years working in an office building? In Minneapolis? Maybe she was interdimensional. Maybe she was a supernatural horror. I'd read enough comic books to have plenty of ideas.

Friday, I decided what to do. We had a birthday cake for Hector, our security manager. As usual, the moment the knife touched the icing, a couple dozen visitors shuffled into the break room, women from all departments who didn't know Hector and didn't care whose birthday it was, in particular.

Gerta was among them, in no way distinguishable from the two women who accompanied her. They griped about the heaters on their floor, and didn't stop griping until they each had a fat square of cake on a paper saucer. They devoured their pieces, saying little, occasionally glancing at the large remaining body of cake on the table. Gerta's eyes tracked me as I closed the cake box and set it on the bottom shelf of the refrigerator.

Back in our own department, I approached Stacy's cube and whispered, "I know who's been eating your lunch."

Stacy, absorbed in the numbers on her monitor, shrieked and jumped in her chair. She scowled at me over her shoulder.

"Sorry," I said.

"Don't sneak up. What is it?"

"I found out about your lunches."

"Really!" She swiveled around to face me. It was Friday, short-hippie-dress day. I struggled to keep my eyes on her face, feeling embarrassed. "Who is it?" she asked.

"I can't explain. I have to show you."

Her eyes narrowed. "Just give me a name." On her armrest, her hand balled into a fist. "Who's been eating my lunch?"

"Can you hang around after work a few minutes?"

"I'd rather not."

"I know, but you have to see this."

"I don't want to," she said. But she agreed.

"You're kidding, right?" Stacy asked. I was standing inside the supply closet, holding open the door for her. "This is really weird, Dave. You're creeping me out."

"Hurry up," I said. "It's almost five o' clock."

Footsteps approached outside the break room door.

"Come *on*!" I whispered.

Stacy shook her head, then stepped into the supply closet with me. I closed the closet door as the break room door opened.

I thought it was Gerta at first, but it was just a woman who resembled her. She crossed to the fridge, extracted a thermos, and left.

"Dave," Stacy whispered. "Why can't you just tell me?"

"I need a witness."

"A witness? I don't like this..."

"Sh!"

The door opened again. A few more employees gathered lunchboxes and rinsed coffee mugs. By five-fifteen, the break room was as quiet and empty as the rest of the building, like a hive after the bees get smoked out.

"This is stupid," Stacy began to stand up. "I'm gonna go. I have to pee, anyway."

The door opened again. I grabbed Stacy and pulled her down toward me, clapping a hand over her mouth. Her eyes went wide, and she probably decided I was a violent lunatic.

"Shhh!" I whispered. "Just watch. Okay?"

Stacy nodded her head, but the frightened look didn't leave her face. She was rigid, ready to fight back.

Gerta opened the refrigerator door and double-checked that she was alone. She extended her fleshy trunk again, and this time it stretched out until it was nearly three feet long.

Stacy squealed a little, and her hands clamped down on my arm. She'd gone from preparing to claw at my eyes to grabbing me for reassurance, or at least to help keep her balance.

"Shh," I whispered.

Gerta's trunk flipped open the cake box, then snorted up a fat red line of frosting along one edge. Her lips punched into the center of Hector's cake. As she sucked, the cake crumpled in from all sides. She slurped the cake up and away through her trunk. It looked like a snake swallowing a rabbit.

All ten of Stacy's fingernails stabbed into my arm, and I had to bite my lip not to yelp.

Gerta wasn't satisfied. Her trunk scooped up yogurt cups, squeezed them until they burst, then guzzled up the contents. She sucked a forgotten brown-bag lunch until the bag lay flat, then chugged a bottle of ranch dressing, which had the words PROPERTY OF AMY, DO NOT USE!!! written on the label in fat black marker.

"So many carbs," Stacy whispered.

Gerta cleaned out the refrigerator. When she was done, she backed up a few steps and stood in the center of the room. She raised her trunk and ejected a puff of dense yellow smoke.

"What's she doing?" Stacy whispered.

"I don't know."

Then the smell hit us, and my stomach surged. I swallowed back vomit. Stacy blanched and pulled the front of her short hippie dress up over her nose, which actually revealed her hips and her lacy green panties, which I forced myself not to look at. They seemed pretty skimpy for office panties, though.

Gerta belched and burbled, and I could hear splashing sounds deep in her stomach. Her face snapped back into human shape, and she turned around to face the closet where we hid.

Stacy and I held our breath.

Gerta opened her mouth, and it kept opening, as if her jaw had become unhinged. Her mouth expanded into a cavernous red maw lined with a ring of teeth. Then the entire mouth inched forward out of her face, and it looked like she was forming a much larger mouth tube. Maybe one big enough to consume humans.

I looked around for a weapon, but the best I could find was a six-pack of Diet Coke. I worked my fingers into a plastic ring, readying myself to bash the monster with it.

But Gerta backed off. She tilted her head up, and her tongue stretched out several feet and attached to the ceiling. The wormlike tongue segments that had been coiled deep inside her bristled with warts and stiff black hairs.

The tongue towed her body up after it. Her mouth pressed against the ceiling tile like a suction cup. She swayed there for a minute, a four-hundred pound mass of beaded kitten sweater, elastic pants and extra-wide orthopedic shoes, clinging like a lamprey eel at the belly of a fish.

Stacy drew close to me and whispered, "Do you think she knows we're here?"

"I don't know."

"Should we go?"

"Not yet," I whispered.

So we waited, huddling together in the dark, looking up at the bizarre monstrosity dangling between the fluorescent bars.

"What do you think it is?" I asked Stacy.

"I don't know," she said. "But it's a lunch thief."

Time did not move. We sat and watched, and eventually my legs fell asleep again. Stacy clung to me, and I don't know what made me more nervous, her bare legs against my khakis or the alien monster.

"I think it's sleeping," Stacy whispered.

Then Gerta pulsed. It was like she was taking deep breaths, her whole body expanding and then shrinking. The pulses intensified, the legs and arms collapsing a little with each deflation, ballooning with each inflation.

Finally, Gerta exploded. Sweater beads fired off in every direction like bullets, ricocheting from the walls and linoleum floor. Her body burst like a water balloon, dripping a rancid fluid that reeked of rotten eggs.

Stacy puked onto my shoulder. She got some inside my shirt collar, too.

Two gray masses the size of beach balls dropped along with the foul water. They unrolled as they hit the ground. They were translucent, with shadowy muscles and organs visible behind their skin. They looked like jellyfish arranged in the rough shape of human beings.

Each had a long trunk, which they immediately used to suck the rotten-egg fluid from the floor. They scrambled around on all fours, first devouring all remnants of Gerta, leaving nothing for the janitorial crew to find. Then they headed for the coffee pot and slurped down the sugar, the powdered creamer, and an entire bucket of Folgers ground coffee.

They were ravenous.

Stacy squeezed both my hands. I'd long since abandoned my

brilliant plan to use a six-pack of soda as a bludgeon.

After they'd consumed everything in the room, the two creatures stopped in the middle of the floor. They touched the palms of their hands together, and their translucent skin rippled. Clouds of flesh-colored pigment flowed within their bodies, and their loose shapes contracted. Their trunks drew inward towards their faces.

One moment, I might have been looking at a pair of giant, hideous amoebas. The next, they were a naked, hairless man and woman, their palms touching. Then a suit and tie formed on the man's body, and a pastel pantsuit with a pearl brooch formed from the woman's skin.

He looked like a low-level executive with male pattern baldness and a beer gut, while she resembled a bland administrative assistant in her mid-thirties, not much makeup, hair pulled into a tight bun. She even wore glasses.

They broke their hand contact and blinked at each other.

At last, the man raised his hand, index finger extended.

"I…would…like…to create…a PowerPoint," he said.

"Yes, sir." A bubble of translucent skin rose from her hand like a balloon, then resolved into a Palm Pilot.

"Title it: Restructuring Hierarchical Management," he said. "Proactive Solutions for an Emerging Paradigm."

The secretary typed. He continued dictating, his words in pure native corporate-speak, his thoughts pre-arranged into bullet points. They left the break room, probably off to colonize a corner office somewhere.

Stacy and I stared at each other for a long time. When we decided it was safe, we scrambled out of the closet.

Stacy faxed in her resignation. I kept the job at Deuschenhoffer for fifteen months, until I moved to Chicago. I never saw Stacy again.

I never saw Gerta's spawn again, either. Something tells me they moved on from manufacturing, perhaps into insurance or finance. They seem to be evolving.

As I move through the corporate world, I find myself wondering how many of them are out there, playing Solitaire, or lingering in the break room, grouching about their foot and back pain. I wonder where they came from, and how they adapted so quickly to our environment, living off coffee, stolen lunches and abandoned fruitcake.

I've never seen one again, as far as I know, but every time I hear an administrative assistant gush about her favorite chocolate cream pie recipe, or an executive sermonize about the need to strategize outside the box to meet a dynamic market environment, I wonder.

I just hope they don't start taking over the IT departments.

Spectrum

from *The Knoxville Observer*:

DIXIE LEE JUNCTION, TN—A meteroid crashed into a
Shoney's parking lot at 7:15 PM, destroying cars and the
Shoney's sign itself, while dozens of diners were enjoying the
buffet.

"It was just a big whizz-dang-doo!" explained Corbelle
Moobley, an eyewitness. She had just exited the Shoney's
with her two daughters, Krystal and Karrie (7 and 9), when the
object passed through her Chevrolet and several other cars
before making a green, gas-filled crater behind the Shoney's.
"It left a big smokey ditch right through the parking lot.
Things was all melty and black. I'm having a heck of a time
with the insurance and all."

"The lights went out, and the whole Shoney's filled right
up with an awful green glow," recalled Mikey Stephens, 48, an
auto mechanic who was eating dinner with an unidentified
young woman. "Then wham! That thing hit the parking lot,
and your spaghetti jumped right off your plate. Spilled my
iced tea, too. Never did get my refill."

Police and firefighters were called to the scene, but they
handed it over to Homeland Security and experts from the
National Institute of Exploratory Science, dispatched from the
federal research facility at Oak Ridge. The entire area was
sealed, with assistance from the National Guard, for more than
twenty-four hours while NIES trucks drove in and out.

"The object in question was simply a large, unstable
rock," said Dr. Gabrielle Hernandez, a special projects
manager at NIES. "It was coated in a layer of volatile
chemicals that ignite in the presence of oxygen. That's why
you hear reports of burning green gas. We've since removed

the object from the crater behind the Shoney's, and health authorities are checking for any lingering hazards."

Shoney's franchise owner Asif Patel plans to rebuild. "I will be open for business as soon as the government lets me repair the parking lot," he said. "When that happy day comes, please try one of our early bird dinner specials."

Text message from GABBY to EVAN:

Might be in Tenn longer than expected! Insane here! Sorry! Love Gab

NIES Internal Report #XB011 (classified)
FROM: Dr. Gabrielle Hernandez, Special Projects Manager
TO. Dr. Jamal Stephens, Director of Research
RE: Exobiological entity

Dr. Stephens,

The examination of the craft wreckage has been taken over by the Air Force. I can only say that it was small and contained four dead specimens.

One occupant survives. In terms of Earth species, it is most similar to a cephalopod, in particular a giant octopus. It can change color to blend with its surroundings, indicating the presence of chromatophores in its skin. The camouflage is rendered so well as to leave him invisible to the human eye, at times. Complex patterns of color have been observed, and our biologists suggest it may be a form of communication. These patterns are being documented for possible interpretation.

We found that he thrives in saltwater, and as approved by your office, we have furnished a ten thousand gallon saltwater aquarium for his habitat. Gradual introduction of seaweed and primitive ocean creatures has proven successful as a source of nutrition. We have developed his habitat with caution, introducing mollusks and crustaceans, on the hypothesis that the oldest forms of ocean life are likely to be closest to the most common organisms in our universe. He is omnivorous, and thus far our ocean plants and animals seem to provide adequate sustenance.

So the specimen continues to thrive. In response to your concerns, yes, we continue to work on the communication problem. We have yet to observe any sign of hostile intent.

Encrypted Email
FROM: Jamal Stephens, Director of Research, NIES
TO: Edward N. Gruber, Assistant Secretary of Defense
SUBJECT: Oak Ridge developments

Assistant Secretary Gruber,

Update on the Oak Ridge situation. Survivor stabilized. No communication with survivor as yet, but indications this will be possible. However, a timeframe cannot be predicted. Whatever the timeframe may be, it can only be accelerated with additional funding and staff.

The researcher in charge has observed no evidence of hostility, but it is impossible to know the thing's purpose or intent. Additional security measures are requested to keep the situation in lockdown.

The specimen is described as "like a giant octopus." Per instructions, I cannot create or share digital pictures of the specimen.

Email
FROM: Evan Kurbow
TO: Gabrielle Hernandez
SUBJECT: Re: Extended stay in The Secret City...

Are you sure it's going to be MONTHS??

And I do understand. You're ears-deep in some crazy project you can't talk about. That's exciting, isn't it? I'm excited for you. Can't wait until you can come home and tell me about it. Does it have anything to do with that meteor? Just wink once if yes.

I miss you.

Love,
Evan

Lab Journal Entry--
Dr. Gabrielle Hernandez

More observations!

The specimen continues to enjoy its seafood diet, and we've introduced a few species of fish as well. Its ability to mimic other organisms is extraordinary. Through changes in color, texture and shape, it has taken the form of a giant-sized version of the crabs in its tank, as well as a large purple anemone with black spots. Once, it appeared to be a school of strange fish, with transparent skin and bioluminescent internal organs.

This led me to study the mimic octopus of Indonesia. The mimic octopus can imitate a number of species, including poisonous fish, jellyfish and sea snakes. It uses mimicry to hide from predators and to hunt prey in disguise, pretending to be either a harmless species or a potential mate. It is my hypothesis that Spectrum's primitive ancestors may have been similar to the mimic octopus.

Based on our sonograms, Spectrum—that's our nickname for the specimen—Spectrum appears to have no skeleton or hard structure of any kind. Its internal structure must be entirely muscular hydrostats, enabling it to reshape its body at will.

To me, this is logical. Cephalopods are the most intelligent invertebrates, as far as mazes and problem-solving tests can determine. A squid or octopus is up to forty percent neural tissue. Combine that capacity for intelligence with the ability to communicate in a broad spectrum of color, texture and shape, and you have the recipe for a highly advanced species. Even one capable of space travel.

NIES Internal Report #XB033 (classified)
FROM: Dr. Gabrielle Hernandez, Special Projects Manager
TO. Dr. Jamal Stephens, Director of Research
RE: Breakthrough!

Dr. Stephens,

Excellent news. With the new projection screen, we have exposed
Spectrum to images of thousands of species of Earth life. His ability to
mimic is astounding. I have seen him do a very good imitation of a
hammerhead shark, including skin tone and eyes, as well as a bottlenosed
dolphin and a sea turtle. He is able to make any unused portion of his
body invisible, with a flatten-and-camouflage technique against the
pebbled floor of the aquarium.

The chromatophores of his skin must be far more advanced than anything
seen in chameleons and other creatures here on Earth. I continue to
believe they must be an extremely visual species, like us, which gives
hope for higher-level communication.

Rajiv, one of the computer guys, rigged up a simple waterproof remote
control, so now Spectrum can pick what he wants to watch on satellite TV.
His favorite show appears to be *Sesame Street*. He also likes the classical
music channel. When listening to Mozart, he floats at the center of the
tank, all eight arms extended radially, shifting through a gradient of rich
hues.

Rajiv suggests turning the clicker into a mouse, as a way to establish
communication. I think his idea is good.

Email
FROM: Evan Kurbow
TO: Gabrielle Hernandez
SUBJECT: Hello?

You know what today is? It's officially two months since we last talked.
Your birthday's tomorrow. Happy birthday, in case you don't reply.

What's happening? Or is it all so very top secret? Are you ever coming back?

I'm missing you a lot, and I'm worried.

Love,
Evan

Private diary,
Dr. Gabrielle Hernandez

Bureaucracy is stupid.

All we need to do is rig Rajiv's remote into a mouse, and Spectrum can type messages to us. But the director is waiting on approval from Defense. Why is this even a question? We are supposed to be establishing communication. Spectrum watches Big Bird fifteen hours a week, and he has hundreds of kilograms of neural tissue—oh, and he's from a species capable of space travel—you think he might know 26 Roman letters and 10 Arabic numerals by now?

While waiting for approval, I've told Rajiv to go ahead with his idea to create a special keyboard for Spectrum, with large letters and numbers. Rajiv thinks it should be circular, with a ball mouse in the center—don't ask me to repeat his explanation, but it had to with the radial symmetry of Spectrum's cephalopod body.

Anyway, I'm really here to write about what happened tonight.

It was after ten PM—I'd gone to sleep on the cot in my office, too tired to drive home. I awoke to Tchaikovsky, the 1812 Overture, blaring loud enough to vibrate the water inside Spectrum's tank. He likes it that way.

I walked out to see him floating there, his arms and body spread out wide and flat, like he was a sail absorbing the voices and music. He glowed in shimmering whites and blues. It reminded me of starlight through a telescope. I thought he looked beautiful.

When I entered, he began to change. He coiled in on himself, then a few of his tentacles rearranged into a shape like a life-sized human doll. One central tentacle became a slender torso and head, with a blank face, and others became simple, featureless arms and legs. Then the tips of the arms grew fingers, and within about two minutes he'd formed a very realistic imitation of human hands.

From there, the arms and legs gained greater definition, and they flexed at newly formed joints. A clumsy imitation of dark brown hair floated around the head.

The face began to mold itself, denting in to make eye sockets, nostrils, mouth. The face rippled again and again as tiny muscles and chromatophores performed microscopic adjustments.

What emerged was my own face, looking back at it me—my brown eyes, my ugly little nose. Only he made me look beautiful, no blemishes, glowing with a golden inner light. He had rendered my whole body, naked (something he'd never seen, of course! and actually my nipples were a little too big and dark).

I reached out toward my glowing twin, and she reached out to me, mimicking my actions. Our fingers pressed against opposite sides of the aquarium wall, which is supposedly bulletproof and unbreakable.

My own eyes looked into me, and what I saw there was profound sorrow.

Then the other me broke apart into four rock-colored tentacles, and Spectrum drifted back and sank down at the back corner of the tank. He turned invisible against the ground.

Encrypted Email
FROM: Jamal Stephens, Director of Research, NIES
TO: Edward N. Gruber, Assistant Secretary of Defense
SUBJECT: Re: Oak Ridge?

Assistant Secretary Gruber,

We have made tremendous progress.

Our specimen has begun a new level of communication. He is able to display detailed information on his body. He created star maps on his skin to show us his planet of origin. He also provided images of what can only be described as a caravan of "spaceships" traveling across the galaxy. Through a numerical display, we believe he informed us they were traveling at more than 99% of the speed of light.

He has clearly begun to reach out to us, but we have not yet reached the level of full communication using language. We will need a significant increase in resources, including staff and equipment, and additional funding to make use of these achievements and take them to the next level.

Email
FROM: Evan Kurbow
TO: Gabrielle Hernandez
Subject: merry x-mas

Well, almost four months and still no word from you. I'm not getting much help from your spooky employer, either. They just tell me you're "safe and happy."

While you're safe and happy, I thought I'd let you know I ran into my old co-worker, Alicia Harris, at the mall the other day. You remember her, from my company Christmas party three years ago? She asked if I was seeing anyone, and I honestly didn't know what to tell her.

What do you think I should tell her?

Evan

NIES Internal Report #XB033 (classified)
FROM: Dr. Gabrielle Hernandez, Special Projects Manager
TO. Dr. Jamal Stephens, Director of Research

RE: Summary

Dr. Stephens,

As requested, what follows is a condensed background summary of information gathered from Spectrum in the three weeks since he became communicative at a high level.

Spectrum identified his species' planet of origin as lying in orbit around HD 21663 in the Hyades star cluster, 151 light years from Earth. Their crafts move just below the speed of light, and the map of his caravan's trade route along the Orion arm is thousands of light years long.

From this, we might deduce he is part of an interstellar nomadic culture. Because of relativity, thousands of years will have passed on HD 21663 by the time his caravan circles back.

Their most recent stop was at Tau Ceti, and their next more than a hundred light years on. Spectrum was on a craft that suffered a mechanical error, and he ejected with others in a lifeboat craft. Only he survived.

He has no way of contacting the caravan, who are parsecs away by now and accelerating. They will not come back this way for thousands of years. He's a castaway, stranded on Earth.

Private diary,
Dr. Gabrielle Hernandez

So, I got to know Spectrum last night.

He mastered Rajiv's round keypad right away, and then downloaded and customized a text-to-speech program, choosing a pleasant baritone for himself. At Spectrum's direction, Rajiv set up an underwater speaker inside the aquarium, and affixed a microphone and speaker to the outside, so we can now have conversations with him.

Spectrum also spends a lot of time on the internet now, reading and watching video on the projection screen outside his aquarium. He's a fast

reader—he finished *Huckleberry Finn* in eighty-three seconds, and said it
was both funny and sad.

I was working late, trying to write in plain English all the reasons
Spectrum doesn't represent a national security risk, and all the useful
knowledge he could likely share. I heard Nina Simone singing "Mood
Indigo" over the speakers in Spectrum's room, and I worried he was sad.
He had plenty to be sad about.

When he saw me, he rose up from the rocks, where he'd been lying in
what I saw as a brooding fashion, his skin deep colors of blue and black.

He lit up a little when I leaned against the tank.

"Hi, Spectrum."

"Hello." Four of his tentacles knotted together in front of me.

"You're not going to make another sculpture of me, are you?" I asked.

"Hahaha." The computerized voice did a poor imitation of laughter.

The tentacles formed into a human shape, but it was male. He looked like
a handsome man in his early thirties, maybe just a little younger than me.
And healthy and well-built. And totally naked.

"Wow," I said. "Who's that?"

"It is me," he said. "I have assembled a human appearance based on what
is considered aesthetically pleasing in your culture."

"You really have."

"I believe this will facilitate communication by adding a fully human
nonverbal dimension." He smiled, and his dark brown eyes—the same
color as mine—twinkled.

"That's...smart."

"It is how my ancestors hunted fish. Look like them, move like them, and you can get close enough to eat."

"Does that mean you're hunting me right now?"

"Hahaha."

I just stared at him floating there in the tank, amazed at how good his physical mimicry was, in every possible way.

"Why are you working so late tonight?" he asked.

"I have to write a report."

"On what?"

I didn't know if I should tell him, but then I heard myself saying, "On whether you can, um, teach us things."

"What kinds of things?"

"Technology. Things like that."

"Things like that." He looked around the cinderblock room. "What is the purpose of this place?"

"To understand you."

"But why was this facility built?"

"Oh. Back in World War II. For the Manhattan Project."

"Which was?"

"The atomic bomb."

Spectrum frowned and looked at me with his very human eyes. He does actually form real eyes with his own nervous tissue. He can generate and absorb these eyes at will, and possibly other organs, too. Think of the medical advances we might make!

"The world war," he said. "The atomic bomb."

"We seem primitive to you, don't we?"

"As a species, you've only just begun to form your external nervous system," he said. "We picked up your disjointed early broadcasts as we approached Tau Ceti. It was like the bright flickering nonsense on a hatchling's skin."

"I don't understand."

"And your focus is weapons. That is what your employers want to know, isn't it? What weapons do my people have? What weapons can I provide your rulers for their next territory game? Do they ask you this?"

"Yes," I admitted. "But there must be peaceful things you could share. Right?"

"Like a quantum reflector?" Spectrum asked.

"What does that do?"

"Instantaneous communication across the universe," he said. "Matter can't travel faster than light, but information can. There is a vast interstellar culture here in our own galaxy, sharing ideas, science, music and art. Anyone with a quantum reflector can tune in."

"That's amazing!" I said. "And you can tell us how to build one?"

"Oh, no. I'm not a quantum engineer."

"What are you?"

"I specialize in the cultivation and exchange of new and exotic plant species," he said.

"You're a...florist?"

"My interests extend well beyond angiosperms! I once created a carnivorous plant to sell as a home security system."

"I guess that's kind of amazing, too."

"Not really. They were too hard to program. Sometimes ate the wrong person."

"Oh."

"These are my favorites." The human shape blew apart, and Spectrum reformed into a garden of giant flowers shaped like origami birds, with brightly colored petals as plumage. "Their name would translate to 'songflowers.'"

"They're beautiful."

"They attract certain species of male songbirds to mate with them." Spectrum created a brightly plumaged bird that swooped down to a flower and began humping it. I had to laugh.

"And some of the songflowers evolved into carnivorous songflowers." A spiny clamshell of a plant mouth slammed shut over the humping songbird. "Which is where I got my bad idea."

A few of his tentacles swirled together and formed the image of the handsome, naked man again. It happened so fast—I think once he takes on a shape, he has the muscle memory to take it again with a thought. He has a thick neural cord through each of his eight arms, plus a massive brain at his core. Every inch of him thinks and feels. And mimics.

"What do you want to do now?" I asked. "If you're stuck on Earth?"

"I'd like to visit the ocean," he said. "Stretch my arms. Play with some creatures. My species depends on both visual and tactile communication. I'm cut off here in the tank. It's like being deaf, for one of you."

"I didn't know that. Would you like more animals brought in? A bigger tank?"

"If that's the best you can do."

"What else do you want?"

He rose toward the top of the aquarium, where the hatch was locked and sealed with titanium bars. The remaining mass of his body remained invisible, blending with the dark wall behind the aquarium.

"Swim with me," he said.

"I'd get fired if I did that!"

"All will be well."

"No, I mean I can't unlock your tank without the director's approval. Major security breach."

"Then I am a prisoner?" He gave a sly smile. "Not merely an honored guest from elsewhere in the galaxy?"

"I guess so. I'm just not authorized--"

"There is no true authority, Gabrielle," he said. "Only when you recognize this, will you put an end to your wars."

"But..." I looked at the steps bolted to the wall beside the aquarium. I knew the combination for the access panel (not that I'm supposed to, but I'm nosy that way). "My job."

"Your job is to establish and maintain communication with me," he said. "What if I went silent and gray for a few days instead?" He crumpled into one corner, looking like an octopus again, and turned the color of a dead spider. "Hahaha."

"That's not funny."

He jetted to the top of the tank again and resumed his human shape. "There are two feet of air on top of the water," he said. "You can swim comfortably."

I can't say why I listened to him, only that I had been so fascinated by him, so consumed by the desire to understand him, that maybe it had given him some sort of power over me. Or maybe I just like him. Anyway, I kicked off my shoes and walked up the stairs. Each step had a rectangular slip-resistant rectangle that scratched against the soles of my feet.

I keyed in the access code. The panel slid open.

He swam up to meet me, reaching his head up out of the water. I tensed, part of me ready for him to attack, or try to push me aside and escape. I thought I understood him now—but you can always be wrong.

"Come on." His voice rippled from the underwater speakers inside his tank. He dove deep. "See my rocks. My crabs."

And yeah, I laughed. And yeah, I'm crazy, but I stripped down to my underwear, and I dove into the tank.

And that's all I'm writing tonight.

FROM: Evan Kurbow
TO: Gabrielle Hernandez
SUBJECT: Re: Sorry about everything...

That's it? You disappear for six months, now you're pregnant? And not mine? Am I clear?

And yes, I have been "banging Alicia Harris like I always wanted anyway." SO WHAT? You ran out on me. You loved your work more. And clearly you haven't been missing me much.

-E

Encrypted Email
FROM: Jamal Stephens, Director of Research, NIES
TO: Edward N. Gruber, Assistant Secretary of Defense
SUBJECT: Re: Re: What kind of zoo are you people running?

Assistant Secretary Gruber,

Yes, we can confirm, with attached Ob/Gyn report, that our project manager, Gabrielle Hernandez, has been impregnated by the specimen. Investigation is ongoing to determine how this happened. All indications are that he was able to successfully mimic human spermatozoa, and that the hybrid fetus is viable.

The specimen's physician, marine biologist, and psychologist all agree that a 100,000 gallon tank will be preferred as a humane permanent residence, including certain rock and coral structures as requested by the specimen himself, especially if we are to house two such creatures now.

The course of the hybrid's development is unpredictable, but we will of course require additional staff to monitor Dr. Hernandez during her pregnancy, and to ensure that the new lifeform is provided appropriate medical care and even education, as well as studied carefully. A budget supplemental request, as well as request for expansion of facility, are attached...

Private diary,
Dr. Gabrielle Hernandez

Finally took Jason to the aquarium today.

During his first month of life, he has appeared to be a normal human baby, and the doctors say he's very healthy. They advised against bringing him to swim in the aquarium—forbid it, actually—but I was sneaking the infant over to see his father anyway.

Jason squealed in my arms when he saw the aquarium. A portion of the boulder castle in Spectrum's new, larger tank shifted from gray to black, then pushed up from the rocks. Tentacles formed into Spectrum's man-shape, the one I've come to love so much. He floated towards the wall of the tank, smiling at both of us.

"Bring him in to me," Spectrum's text-to-speech said over the speaker.

"Are you sure? He's too small to swim."

"We will see, Gabrielle."

So I took one backward glance to make sure the door was closed, and then I carried Jason up the steps. I opened the access panel. Spectrum rose waist high out of the water, and I handed him the baby so I could take off my clothes. I swim naked in the tank now (only at night, of course!)— there's no point dealing with soggy, salty underwear.

Of course, everybody here thinks I'm a crazy person.

I jumped into the aquarium and began treading water. Spectrum sank until he was chest-high, and he eased our infant son into the salty water. Jason giggled and kicked his feet.

"Careful," I said. "You can't expect him to swim yet."

Then Jason's skin color changed to black and white zebra stripes. His arms and legs unfurled into a four-point star shape. Then he slipped out of Spectrum's hands and dove deep into the tank, pumping water behind him, as if his entire month as a human baby had been nothing but mimicry. He looked like a four-armed octopus as he crawled onto the boulder castle, turned gray, and vanished.

"He's not really human?" I asked.

"He's both of us." Spectrum coiled his arms around me. "He is something new."

I watched Jason chase a school of seahorses. As he played, he turned into a giant, lumpy, crude imitation seahorse himself.

His fish-mimicry skills need work, but he's a great swimmer.

THE FIXER

Norton picked up the fixer at the company's private airfield north of the city. The airfield didn't directly belong to Norton's specific employer, Dynamatx International, but rather to the parent conglomerate HHK.

Norton had imagined the fixer as a giant of a man, the type who could crush your skull like a Dixie cup in one fist, but the man was instead thin, pale, and even a little shorter than Norton. Norton felt big and clumsy next to him. The fixer reclined in Norton's passenger seat and kept his face neutral behind solid black data glasses.

As Norton drove away from the airfield, he glanced with some guilt at the wad of cellophane bunched up in the cupholder of his Buick. The coffee cake had left a smudge of white icing on the cellophane. He imagined himself through the fixer's eyes—fat and soft, his stomach bulging visibly beneath his tie, glasses so thick they magnified his eyes to cartoony size.

Norton wondered if the fixer, or his boss, knew about the accounts in China. And what would happen to Norton if they did.

"How many?" the fixer asked. He set his brushed titanium briefcase on the floor between his Armani loafers.

"Excuse me?" Norton said.

"Targets. I was told eight. Is that correct?"

"Yes, sir," Norton said. "I mean, yeah, eight, far as I can tell. Look, this is not really, I mean I don't work in security. I'm in the accounting department. I don't have experience with this kind of thing, is what I'm saying."

"They told me you could finger the targets." the fixer spoke in a soft, low voice.

"Targets?"

"Those with their hands in the cookie jar."

"Right," Norton said. "Well, I did uncover the cash flow anomalies, and I did the initial forensics on the missing money. So I've been in the middle of the investigation. I'm just not clear exactly what your role is going to be here."

"You drive me to the targets. I deal with them."

"That's what I'm fuzzy about."

The fixer cocked his head. For a moment, Norton thought he looked like some kind of bird, the kind that sweeps down in the night to snatch prey in its talons. The fixer said nothing.

They drove down the interstate toward the city. Someone had strung the streetlamps with plastic wreaths and garlands. Norton flipped through the radio stations, finding mostly Christmas carols. Snow the color of dark ash littered the road.

"Have you visited Detroit before?" Norton asked.

"No reason to."

"That's what everyone says."

"Mind if I smoke?" the fixer asked.

Norton did. He minded very much. Even the smell of a cigarette across the room irritated his asthma. "Go ahead," he said.

The fixer lit up a Marlboro, then cracked the window half an inch, maybe less. Norton's stomach heaved.

"How much did these guys take?" the fixer asked.

"I can verify sixty-two million dollars," Norton said. "They've run a pretty complex operation. The tech guys said they found a tangle of unauthorized programs in our transaction software."

"I heard eighty million," the fixer said.

"Could be more," Norton said. "A lot more. We're still unraveling things."

"You'd think somebody would notice sooner."

"Dynamatx handles trillions of dollars in transactions per year," Norton said. "All they need is somebody inside the company to cover it up. One or two key people."

"If there are, you might have made enemies blowing the whistle," the fixer said. "Ever think of that?"

Norton hadn't, and the thought disturbed him. He suddenly wished he had another of the coffee cakes. And a coffee, too, with plenty of sugar. It was almost midnight, and Norton was no night owl. "I was just doing my job," he said.

"Dangerous job."

"But it isn't! I just strap into my interface chair all day. Nobody talks to me. Now it's all conference rooms where everybody's whispering, then asking me questions, then whispering."

"Sounds exciting."

"I just want it to be over," Norton said. "It's Christmas Eve, for God's sake. I should be at home with my—with my tree, watching the Grinch or something."

The fixer grunted and looked out the window.

The thieves had penetrated Dynamatx from an office in a rundown, half-empty professional park, in a district cluttered with empty warehouses. The professional park turned out to be two rows of cinderblock buildings facing each other across a parking lot, their narrow lawns crawling with weeds, the whole facility encircled by barbed chainlink. The front gate hung open, and the fixer instructed Norton to drive on through.

"Where?" the fixer asked.

"Suite 130."

"Park across from that."

Norton did, pulling into a space in front of a black glass door. The letters stenciled on the door in fading, chipped gold paint read: "An ie Mel urne, Tr v l Ag nt."

The fixer opened his steel briefcase. He withdrew a small black box and lifted the lid, revealing what looked to Norton like three darts resting on black velvet.

The fixer opened a palmtop in his briefcase and tapped at the keys. The three darts unfolded little paperclip mechanical legs and trundled in a perfect circle around the black velvet. Waxy wings unfurled from their backs, and the bugs lifted into the air.

They flew out of the passenger window and spiraled toward the building's air conditioning intake.

"This is your part," the fixer said. "Confirm the guys. That's all you have to do."

The fixer turned the screen of his palmtop toward Norton. It displayed the viewpoint of each bug.

They peered through air vents into offices piled with takeout boxes, soda cans, overflowing ashtrays. The hackers were not even divided into cubicles, but sat at workstations on long, cluttered tables along the walls. They were mostly male, not one of them over the age of thirty.

In the movies, they would have had punk haircuts and strange body piercings, but these guys had more of a rumpled business-casual look. They each sat back in their cheap office chairs, with black cups over their eyes, expensive Indian input sensors stretched over their fingertips like tiny yellow condoms. Each man was lost in his own world, swiveling his head, twitching his fingers in midair, muttering quietly.

"Is it them?" the fixer asked.

"It must be," Norton said. "The unauthorized transactions were directed from here. I identified eight users—here there's six, seven…eight."

"Perfect," the fixer said. He opened a panel inside his briefcase and slipped out a boxy machine pistol. He fed it an ammunition clip, then dropped more clips inside his jacket.

"Wait a minute--" Norton said.

"Keep the motor running," the fixer said. "It'll only take a second."

"I can't do this," Norton said. "I told you, I'm not in the security department or anything like that—"

"Don't worry about it. Look, you can sing a little Christmas carol while I'm gone." The fixer got out and eased the door closed. He pointed a slender remote-control wand, the size of a black pencil, at Norton's car. Norton's radio cranked up until "The Little Drummer Boy" played at ear-splitting volume. The fixer smiled.

Norton watched the fixer cross the broken asphalt parking lot and try the door to 103. Locked. The fixer raised the machine pistol, blasted through the door handle, then walked inside.

Norton heard another shot five seconds later, followed by the sound of a woman screaming. Or it could have been a very frightened young man.

"Our finest gifts we bring, pah-rum-pum-pum-pum," Norton sang with the radio. "To lay before the King, pah-rum-pum-pum-pum…" A rattling chain of shots thundered inside the building. A stray bullet burst through one window, and Norton's sideview mirror exploded. He gasped and scrunched down in his seat.

There was a lull, and then one kid who looked about eighteen, with shaggy hair and a scraggly beard, burst through the black front door clutching a briefcase to his chest. The fixer stepped out of the shattered door after him, raised the pistol, fired one shot. The briefcase ruptured, spilling thousands of silver data discs the size of nickels, as if the kid was a slot machine that had just paid off big.

The kid fell to his knees. The fixer grabbed him up and dragged him back into the office. The open briefcase still clutched in the kid's hand spilled the iridescent nickels across the black ice of the parking lot. These rolled along the snail trail of the kid's blood.

"I have no gift to bring, pah-rum-pum-pum-pum," the radio sang.

"That's fit to give our King, pah-rum-pum-pum-pum…"

More shots thundered inside the building. There was a pause, and then two more shots.

The fixer emerged and strolled back to the car. He was empty-handed, which seemed wrong to Norton.

"Where's your gun?" he asked whens the fixer dropped into the passenger seat.

"Thing's a murder weapon now," the fixer said. "I don't want it. Do you?"

Norton shook his head.

"Drive."

Norton drove.

The fixer raised his thin black wand and pressed an unmarked button on the side. The office park erupted into a column of fire that filled Norton's rearview mirror.

"I played my best for Him," the fixer sang along. "Pah-rum-pum-pum-pum, rum-pum-pum-pum, rum-pum-pum-pum…"

Norton parked at the airfield. His hands shook against the steering wheel. It had been a very quiet drive. The dark airfield lay deserted for the holidays, behind layers of electrified fences and coiled barbed wire, the grounds patrolled only by remote-controlled armored bots. All the windows in the hangars and the hospitality building were dark and empty.

"Here we are," Norton said. He couldn't wait for the man to get out of his car, as well as his life. "Merry Christmas. Very nice to meet you. Maybe we'll work together again sometime."

The fixer touched his black data glasses.

"Home office," the fixer said. "Wait here. He might want to talk to you."

"Who?"

"Jacques bin Faisal." The fixer climbed out of the car and slammed the door.

Norton sat back and tried to breath. He found his inhaler in his glove box and took a deep pull. Jacques bin Faisal, of the Saudi-French banking dynasty, was the current chairman of the HHK board in Jeddah. If the man decided Norton had done a good job, Norton could move into a very successful career. If not…Norton began to tremble.

He watched the airfield. After he'd waited a painfully long time, a sleek black V-shaped jet dropped from the sky, rolled a short length down the runway, then came to an abrupt halt. The black jet moved in a way that reminded Norton of a woolly spider that had fallen on him from the ceiling fan, the summer his parents had rented the condo on the Jersey shore.

The hangar door opened as the plane approached, but the interior of the hangar remained dark. That didn't stop the black plane from crawling on in.

The fixer appeared at Norton's window like a ghost. He waved for Norton to get out of the car.

"What is it?" Norton asked.

"Your lucky night," the fixer said. "Jacques wants to see you immediately."

"I have to go to Saudi Arabia?"

"Manhattan."

"But I'm not prepared…" Norton looked down at his old, partially unraveled cardigan sweater. He didn't have a change of clothes with him.

"You'll be fine."

"But it's Christmas Eve—"

"He's Muslim. And an absurdo-atheist. That's the French half."

Norton hesitated, but he didn't see much of a choice. He locked up his car and followed the fixer to a gate in the inner fence surrounding the landing field.

"After you," the fixer said. The gate beeped and slid aside. Norton glanced up at the cluster of smooth black spheres hung like grapes above the gate. At least one member of the security staff would be on duty, somewhere on the planet, watching them in realtime. Or at least automated realtime anomaly aggregates spit out by video content analysis software.

Norton stepped through the gate. The gravel lawn of the landing field crunched under his wide feet. It might have been the only sound for miles.

The fixer followed, and again, he moved like a cat on padded feet, making no sound. The man's complete silence unnerved Norton. The fixer could be on top of him in an instant, if he meant to kill Norton, too.

"Wait," the fixer said. Norton turned back and saw him coughing into one gloved hand. The man looked a little paler than before, and somehow smaller. "Think I picked up a cold. Woke up in the desert this morning. Now I got Jack Frost up my ass." He coughed again, louder, ringing out like a gunshot in the cold night.

"I think it's colder in New York," Norton said.

"I'll just stay on the plane."

Norton was disappointed when he saw their plane. The sleek black craft that had pounced in earlier wasn't for them. Instead, they boarded a chubby-looking unmarked jet. Inside, the upholstery was threadbare, badly stained, and pockmarked with burns.

"Problem?" the fixer asked. He took a seat by a window and set his briefcase between his feet.

"It's not what I was expecting," Norton said.

"Still beats flying commercial."

Norton shrugged. He picked a seat in one of the few rows without any of the big, dark stains.

After a minute, a screen at the front of the plane flickered, and then showed a man in a pilot's cap who sported an overgrown handlebar mustache.

"Captain here. Looks like you're my only passengers," he said. "Buckle in and we'll get moving. We've got a mostly clear night, a little snow around New York, but   easy sailing ahead. Maybe you guys can enjoy a white Christmas."

"Thanks," Norton said. The screen blacked out.

He actually felt better once they were airborne. If the fixer intended to kill Norton, he could have done that on the ground. This seemed a little elaborate for one murder, considering the fixer's demonstrated murdering-sociopath skills. Norton turned to speak to the fixer, who sat several rows back.

"Do they have drinks on these planes?" Norton asked.

"Oh, yeah. Gorgeous stewardesses, too. But not for us, as you see."

"Just drinks, then?"

"Check the galley up front."

Norton unbuckled and walked up the aisle. He found a refrigerator cabinet stocked with large bottles of Macallan's Scotch and Suntory Yamazaki single-malt.

"You want one?" he called back to the fixer.

"Sure."

"Yamazaki?"

"Anything's fine."

Norton poured two whiskeys. He didn't drink much, but this was clearly one of those times that called for it.

He carried them back to the fixer, who had a large, unsettling smile. Norton handed him the cup, but it tumbled right through the fixer's fingers, then through his leg, and then splattered across the seat. Norton gaped.

"Sorry, friend," the fixer said.

"What is this?" Norton passed his hand through the fixer's head.

"Hologram," the fixer said. "I'm still back at the airfield, I'm afraid."

"I don't understand."

"This plane is not going to New York," the fixer said. "We're going to fly out over the Atlantic for about a thousand miles. Then this plane will be lost in the ocean. So will you. It's nothing personal."

"But…" Norton looked out at the black sky with a rising sense of panic. "Does the pilot know? What's he going to do?"

"You mean this guy?" The fixer nodded at the video screen, and the mustached pilot's face appeared again.

"…a little snow around New York, but it's no problem. Maybe you guys can enjoy a white Christmas." The video froze on the pilot's goofy grin.

Norton jumped to his feet and stumbled to the front of the plane. He opened the cockpit door, but the cockpit was shielded by a hard plastic wall. Both pilots' chairs were folded down into compartments in the floor.

Norton was alone on the plane.

He returned to the cabin, where the hologram of the fixer now stood in the aisle, watching him.

"Why are you doing this?" Norton asked.

"I told you, poke your head up, make enemies. Like you said, there had to be insiders to cover up that much missing cash. Sixty million, right? Or was it eighty? A hundred?"

"But I was just doing my job!"

"So am I," the fixer said. "It's when we step outside our little roles things get dangerous. You did that to yourself."

Norton stared at the night outside. "But why waste an entire airplane on me?"

"Yeah, the plane. We've had some pretty intense off-the-book activities up here. More of an embarrassment at this point. We have to juggle it from city to city, make sure none of the board get a look at it. You can imagine how they'd react."

"So you're not with the board of directors. You weren't talking to Jacques bin Faisal."

"No, but I am a good friend of your regional manager. He intercepted your report."

Norton slumped into a bloodstained seat. He noticed the whiskey in his hand and sipped it. He winced and clenched his teeth as the burn scoured its way down to his stomach, where it exploded in a ball of heat. Norton coughed and wheezed.

The fixer appeared in the seat beside him.

"They're going to blame me, aren't they?" Norton said. "Tell the board I was embezzling—"

"The heat came down, you panicked, stole a company plane…" the fixer said. "Crashed into the Atlantic. We planted a whole data wake behind you, flight simulator programs, crap like that. You put a down payment on a twenty-million-dollar house in Martinique. That's where you were trying to go. Only you're an idiot and got lost."

Norton ran to the plastic wall of the cockpit. He couldn't find any way to open it, so he just pounded it with his fists.

The fixer appeared beside him. "Oh, come on. Even if you could get in there, would you really know what to do? You'd only finish my job for me."

"I could call someone."

"Nope. Stripped the voice. There's no flight recorder, no transponder, no emergency beacon, and definitely no parachutes, so don't bother. You should really try to relax. Help yourself to the drinks. Good appetizers in the fridge, usually."

"Thanks."

Norton fidgeted. He paced the aisle. He sipped his drink and tried to swallow back the burn. He finished it off and set it into a cupholder on an aisle seat.

The fixer materialized beside him. "Want me to play Christmas music or anything?"

"Are you planning to hang around here until I die?" Norton looked at the fixer with what he really hoped was a fierce, intimidating glare.

"I have to see the job through."

"That's nice." Norton continued pacing.

"Silver Bells" played over the airplane's sound system.

Norton stopped pacing.

"There's more money," he said.

The hologram of the fixer turned back from the window, where he'd been looking out at the stars. "What?"

"They can't pin down how much is missing. I've tracked sixty-one million for them. I know about seventeen million more that I never…I never reported."

The fixer regarded him carefully, then a smile broke across his face.

"Don't tell me you squirreled away all that money for yourself," the fixer said. "I reviewed your profile. You're not that proactive. 4Q personality. Submissive."

"I didn't do it," Norton said. "It was the, it was those hacker guys you killed. Some of them were running an inside game against the others. I didn't report it."

"You're bluffing."

"Most of the money was distributed around the Caribbean," Norton said. "But some went into coded accounts in Asian banks."

"And why did you fail to report this?" the fixer asked.

"I was still investigating how they arranged the transfers. Now I'm the only person left alive who knows how to access those accounts. You even blew their computers to hell."

The fixer stared at him.

"We can split it," Norton said. "A holiday bonus for both of us."

"Wait a minute," the fixer said. "Let me think this over."

Norton waited. "Silver Bells" became "Blue Christmas," as performed by Porky Pig.

The fixer finally spoke. "I should get eighty percent."

"What?"

"I'd be disobeying orders," the fixer said. "Could be my head on the slab real quick."

"Okay," Norton said.

"Give me the accounts first, so I know you're not lying."

Norton thought it over. "I'll give you one. Royal Bank of Thailand—can you access from there?"

The fixer nodded. His fingers pointed in midair, at a menu Norton couldn't see.

"0089314-34525," Norton said. He'd memorized all of them. Just in case. "Password OMAHA7948."

The fixer scratched his nose, then shook his head.

"There's only six hundred thousand here," he said.

"The smallest account," Norton said.

"Give me more."

"Not a chance," Norton said.

The fixer stared at him. Norton stared back.

"Just one second." The fixer tapped his fingertips in the air. "We don't want you landing at any HHK airfield. I'm bringing you down on a strip outside Tomahawk, Wisconsin. Wait for me on the plane. Do not get off. I'm flying over to meet you."

"Good." Norton buckled in.

When the plane landed, Norton walked past the hologram of the fixer, which sat inanimate as a discarded puppet in the seat by the door. The fixer himself was focused on flying his own craft, probably the black spidery plane. Norton had no intention of waiting here for the man.

He opened the exterior door, and watched the stairs automatically uncurl to the ground. Then he reconsidered. The fixer would track him down eventually. Norton had a strong suspicion that the fixer was the sort of man who would take him to a dark, underground place and torture him for weeks until he gave up the money.

Norton couldn't find any paper, but he found a black permanent marker clipped to the back of a passenger seat. He wrote account numbers and passwords on the stained, filthy wall just inside of the door, so the fixer couldn't miss them. They were from the People's Bank of Beijing, and banks scattered throughout the industrial cities along the coast of China. Norton wrote the names of the banks in Chinese ideograms. He saved back only one relatively small account for himself.

Then he added the words "Merry Christmas!" He underlined these words twice.

He sucked chemical mist from his inhaler, then stepped out into the winter night.

Bad Code

Before Donald Patello awoke, he traveled in endless loops through the shifting three-dimensional labyrinth of Triod Consolidated, LLC's financial structure.

Boxy icons representing assets, some of them as large as city blocks, depreciated slowly, melting like ice cubes on a cool autumn day. Revenue streams--sometimes a trickle, sometimes a torrent--circulated from one subsidiary to another. Small tributaries drained off into black tax holes wherever a revenue stream crossed a political boundary.

Self-awareness struck him suddenly and completely, as if he'd jolted awake from a long, bad dream. How long had he been plugged into Triod's central database, scrutinizing the multinational operations? Hours? Days?

As a young programmer, he'd worked himself beyond exhaustion this way, trying to adjust every minor detail, complete that next task, reach that next step. Absorbed by work, he lost all sense of himself as a human being separate from the dense webworks of information around him. But that was in the distant past.

As the company had grown, Donald spent less and less time in the world of raw data, more time shaking hands and making plans, usually over wine and gourmet meals prepared by the executive chef. Consequently, he'd grown from a scrawny, hyperactive coder into a middle-aged executive with a hefty gut and a face full of broken vessels.

It was unlike him to obsess over these financial minutiae--that was the job of the adaptive AI software Donald had helped create himself, including programs that had eventually yielded Triod billions of dollars. Now he felt caught in the sort of bad dream that had him back in school, horribly late for the final exam of a class he'd never attended.

He thought of his family, and the digital environment, responding to this new firing of his neurons, generated full-size holograms of them.

His wife Becki, much younger and far more athletic than him, floated in a spotless white tennis outfit, including the diamond bracelet she'd insisted he purchase for their first anniversary. Their daughter Nina, just eight years old but full of easy, confident smiles, twirled in her ballet costume, her hair tied back with lavender ribbon.

Guilt washed over Donald, eating him inside and out, as if he'd committed some unspeakable crime against his family, the specifics of which he just could not remember.

He summoned a calendar, saw that it was August 28, 2071, 3:27:18 AM. He was extremely late. Panicking, he realized that he could not remember the last time he'd talked to Becki and Nina, whether it had been hours or days. He could not remember when he'd plugged into the central database. Time came crashing down on him, and he was suddenly, painfully aware how badly he'd been neglecting his family.

With a mental flick of his hand, Donald collapsed the cityscape of data into a small configuration of glowing geometrics. He logged out of the company network and headed home.

Donald felt dazed as he stood in the dark two-story foyer of his apartment, the steel-ribbed cloned-maple door sealed behind him. The lights failed to notice his presence, and he didn't bother telling them to illuminate. He'd lived in the apartment for a decade, since marrying Becki. Before that, he'd still lived in the cramped studio he'd rented during his first grunt job at Triod, despite having accrued many millions in options in the intervening years. He simply hadn't bothered to move, too busy with work. Becki, though, needed a much bigger, nicer place, one lined with marble and decorated by the trendiest designers, a home that made it clear she was no longer just a recruiting assistant at Triod.

He moved up the stairs, feeling numb all over, dissociated from his body, the way he always felt after losing track of time inside a digital environment. He couldn't remember ever being so happy just to come home.

He looked into Nina's room first, and saw his daughter sleeping under the dim, rapidly pulsing glow of a hologram floating above her bed. Probably one of her cartoons. Donald moved in for a closer look, and saw that Nina had drowsed off to sleep watching, not zany cartoon animal antics, but a music video of a band he didn't recognize.

A gang of young men with a patchwork of sensor pads pasted to their bare bodies crashed and bumped against each other, bits of music apparently resulting whenever two sensor pads touched. The volume was barely above hearing level, but the noise was cacophonous and chaotic enough that Donald waved away the hologram. He deleted it for good measure--Nina was still too young to start the boy-band obsessions, in his opinion.

The sudden loss of light and sound caused Nina to stir in her bed, and Donald noticed that, instead of her Punky Pony blanket with its paint-splotch-polka-dot design, she slept under a Tiffany blue comforter with lace trim. Her bed had lost most of its stuffed animals and accumulated dainty throw pillows in their place.

Nina's eyes opened, staring into the empty place where the band had been.

"Nina?" Donald whispered. As he spoke, a little illumination rose around him, the room responding to activity. The entire color palette of her room had changed, from vivid pinks and yellows to muted pastels.

The biggest change, though, was Nina herself. As she looked at him, he saw that her black hair was much longer, her cheekbones more defined, her nose fuller--her whole body seemed longer, as if she'd grown a foot or more.

Nina was a teenager.

Her eyes widened at the sight of him. A look of terror crept into her face.

"Nina, what's wrong?" he asked, moving closer. She drew back against her pillows. Her lips moved against each other, but he had to tune in close to hear the sound:

"*Ohmygod, ohmygod...*"

"Nina?" He reached for her, but she recoiled, trembling. "Nina, what can I do?"

A whisper breathed out of her mouth.

"I'm sorry, what did you say, honey?"

Her lips moved again, very slightly, but this time he understood her.

"*Go away.*"

Donald reeled back into the hall, confused and disoriented. How could Nina have grown so much? Why was she scared of him? Again, he felt the deep guilt of too much time away from his family--but surely it hadn't been years. That was impossible.

Donald hurtled past the guest rooms and his home office, into the master bedroom. He would wake up Becki. She would provide a rational explanation, such as the fact that this was all a dream, and then *she* would wake *him* up, out in the real world, and his daughter would be her normal self again.

Donald stopped at the foot of the bed, staring.

Becki wasn't alone.

She lay under a large man with a hairy, freckled back, her bronzed thigh squishing into the vast meat roll of his jiggling midsection. She was panting lightly, her eyes closed. He was huffing and grunting into her face.

When the man turned his head aside, Donald recognized the scrunched eyes and clenched teeth of Lubbock McElroy, once famous for his flaring red mane of a beard, now better known for his obvious toupee.

Lubbock had been with Triod almost as long as Donald, since the company was a half-dozen rooms in a seedy Seattle low-rise. They had been teammates, co-developers of the suite of full-immersion financial software that transformed Triod into a global heavyweight. They'd spent endless hours collaborating deep inside the network.

"What's going on here?" Donald asked.

Lubbock continued heaving away on top of Becki, but her eyes flared open and she craned her neck to look over Lubbock's huge, freckled shoulder. She stared at Donald for a very long moment.

Then she screamed.

Lubbock's eyelids fluttered apart, and he turned to see the reason for Becki's scream. At the sight of Donald, he gasped, lost his balance, rolled off the side of the bed and landed hard on the floor. His thick arms and legs flailed out blindly from beneath the heap of blankets he'd dragged with him. He looked like an upturned sea turtle.

"Donald?" Lubbock's muffled voice was weak and oddly high-pitched, almost like a child's. "Donster?"

On the bed, Becki gathered the single remaining sheet around her, folding her knees up to her chest, and stared up at Donald with pain in her eyes.

Despite finding his best friend sleeping with his wife, Donald felt no jealousy or anger, as if someone had switched off the entire reptilian portion of his brain. He did have a strong reaction--a deeper elaboration of the guilt and regret that had broken his concentration inside the database, mixed with fresh confusion. That was all his own fault, his own failure to take care of his family and spend time with them.

He rushed away from the bedroom, down the stairs, and out the door into darkness.

Dr. Suri Bahramzadah, psychiatric counselor in Triod's human resources department, glared at her administrative assistant through a two-d projection of her daily calendar, which floated as a transparent rectangle above her assistant's desk.

"Is this a joke?" Suri demanded.

"No, ma'am," replied Suri's assistant Molly Yu, a heavyset woman who seemed to own a wardrobe full of canary yellow pantsuits. Molly frowned as she studied the text inside the holographic gridlines. "I didn't…schedule it. I don't know how it got there."

"Sorry. My fault." Donald approached them from the 80th-floor elevator lobby, giving his best apologetic smile. He was trying desperately to keep it together, put up a casual appearance.

Molly and Suri turned, and they both fell silent, gaping at him.

"I saw an open hour and added my name," Donald explained. Neither of them reacted. "I hope that's all right. I'm…it's a little bit of an emergency."

"Yes," Suri said. She didn't move, her expression did not change, and she seemed almost unaware she'd spoken.

Everyone seemed afraid of Donald, and he didn't know why. He'd spent twenty minutes examining himself in a mirror down in the lobby, and couldn't find anything visibly wrong with his face or body.

He passed Suri and entered the open door of her office, which was a spare, white environment with a soft organic shape, no straight lines or corners at the walls. To one side of him stood a fountain, where a thin sheet of water poured over shelves of pebbles, creating a soothing, trickling sound. Ripe green herbs grew in a window box mounted beside it. He turned back to look at Suri, who still hadn't budged from her place in front of Molly's desk, though she and Molly continued staring at him.

"Are you coming?" he asked. "Sorry again about the short notice."

"Yes…Mr. Patello. Go ahead. One moment." Suri leaned down to Molly and whispered very softly, but Donald found he could listen in close despite the gurgling fountain. She whispered: "*Tell no one about this. And delete his name from my calendar*."

"Yes, ma'am." Molly plucked Donald's name from the holographic calendar with her fingers, and it dissolved, leaving a fading puff of digital dust in the air. Then she jabbed a fist through the calendar, and it vanished.

"…so I don't know what any of it means, or what I'm supposed to do," Donald said. He'd explained his recent problems to the best of his abilities. Suri, a tiny woman, had sat on the front lip of her massively oversized cushion chair, listening to him, her wide, dark eyes hardly blinking as she stared at him.

She'd clenched a light pen in one hand and a palm tablet in the other, but had not made a single note. She'd not said another word, nor asked any questions.

"So..." Donald said, trying to goad her into talking. "I was thinking...maybe it's some kind of amnesia? Maybe I'm too old stay plugged in half the night. Could that be it?"

"I...wouldn't say that is your problem." Suri spoke each word slowly, as if selecting them very carefully. "Would you mind if I bring in someone else to consult?"

"Go ahead."

Suri tapped at her palm screen, her lacquered fingers clacking across the slick surface.

"It will just be a moment," she said to Donald. "Are you comfortable sitting there?"

"I'm fine," Donald said. Suri's couch was upholstered with what appeared to be handmade quilts. He sat in the exact center of it, his hands folded in his lap.

"You were lying down just a moment ago."

"Was I? You're right. I was."

"Until I suggested you were sitting up," Suri said. "Then you were sitting."

"Yes..."

"Do you recall the intervening moment just now? The repositioning of your body between lying and sitting?"

"I...what?" Donald tried to recall sitting up. "Not really. So? What does that mean?"

The room chimed twice, indicating an incoming call. Suri waved her hand, and Lubbock McElroy materialized in the center of the room. His holographic avatar was noticeably slimmer and better groomed than McElroy had ever been in realworld. And it still had the beard.

"What is it, Doctor?" McElroy asked. "We're in a meeting."

Suri nodded at Donald. McElroy turned, and he gaped.

"Oh. Oh." McElroy held up a finger, turned to someone Donald couldn't see. "Sorry, minor emergency on this end. Mind if I call back?"

McElroy studied Donald in silence. McElroy's holographic eyes glowed a supernatural emerald green. For more than a year, McElroy had always appeared in casual online conversation as a werewolf in nut-hugging jogging shorts--the eyes were a remnant of that nearly forgotten era.

"How long have you been sleeping with my wife?" There was no malice in Donald's voice, nor inside of him. It was dispassionate, just a query for needed information.

"Right." McElroy cleared his throat, looked down at Dr. Bahramzadah for guidance.

"Go ahead and answer him," she said.

"Okay...Donald. Becki and I have been together for four..." McElroy again glanced to Dr. Bahramzadah. "...well, maybe four and a half years."

Donald shook his head. "Four years. I never suspected."

"She got pretty upset after you died," McElroy said. Suri shot him a glare, her teeth bared, shaking her head. McElroy either didn't notice or ignored her. "She kept inviting me over...I didn't know what to do, Donald. Woman like that gets what she wants--which I still can't believe turned out to be *me*--but still--she was crying and she was *begging* me--begging *me*, of all the people--"

"Stop," Donald said. "Back up. Right back to that part about 'after I died?'"

"Donald, will you do me a favor?" Suri asked. She lifted a smooth, oyster-colored pebble from her fountain. "Will you hold onto this for me?"

Donald stared at the pebble. It seemed dangerous, like a live coal, something that would burn him. He pulled his hand back from it.

"Lubbock," Donald said. "I don't remember dying."

"Aw, it sucked, man!" McElroy said. "Heart attack. We should never have hired that gourmet chef. Seriously. At the funeral, we had two those Korean spider robots carry your casket--you should have been there." A frown crumpled McElroy's puffy, freckled face. "Everybody misses you. Especially Nina. Took her forever to quit asking when you'd come back home."

"Is he telling the truth?" Donald asked Suri.

She gave a very slight nod, her eyes judging his reaction carefully. "You have been deceased for almost five years, Mr. Patello."

The now-familiar black wave of guilt and regret fell over Donald again. He'd neglected his daughter, and now she had grown up without him. Because he was dead.

Anguish boiled inside him, and he felt himself swell out like a spiked blowfish, stabbing into every corner of the room. The concave ceiling lights sputtered, then two of them burst in a shower of sparks and glass. Angry, painful noise screeched from the hidden speakers tucked into the walls, loud enough that Suri and McElroy covered their ears as they ducked away from the broken glass spilling from the ceiling.

Then it was over, his emotion spent, and Donald collapsed back into himself.

"I warned you about this," Suri snapped to McElroy. "I told you we needed stronger filters--"

"We put in your filters," McElroy yelled back at her. "You screwed them up! This is your fault!"

"We've never had an incident--"

"Wait, wait, wait!" Donald said. "Does anyone want to tell me what we're talking about?"

They both turned to him, startled. Donald's voice had boomed from every side of the room.

"Mr. Patello," Suri said, once again talking as if every word were a calculated choice. "You believe that you are Mr. Patello, correct?"

"Yes…" Donald was not enjoying this turn of the conversation.

"You specialized in artificial intelligence," Suri said. "Specifically, software with the capability of learning from its users, predicting their choices."

Donald nodded. He felt cold inside.

"One such experiment was the program that eventually became the Self-2 Personal Helper."

"It's a software agent," McElroy interrupted. "Designed to offload a portion of an executive's decision-making burden. It begins by studying your neural firing patterns as you go about your workday, then over time it takes on small, routine tasks. As it gets to you know you better, it becomes more capable of predicting your probable decisions. The bond traders love it."

"Donald," Suri said, "*You* are Mr. Patello's agent. The first prototype. Mr. Patello passed on five years ago."

Donald stared at her for several seconds, then shook his head. "That's not possible."

"Take this." Suri held out the smooth pebble again, but Donald jerked away from her. He was suddenly standing on the far side of the room from her, holding up his hands.

"That's not possible," he repeated. "It doesn't have a social-interface function. It wasn't designed for that."

"Actually, we've developed quite an advanced interface," McElroy said. "But you're right, your prototype version didn't have it."

"Then why am I here?" Donald asked. "This doesn't make any sense."

"That's what I need to determine," Suri said. "Donald, could you tell me--what is your first memory? I don't mean from Mr. Patello's life, but more recently. What brought you out into the world?"

Donald thought it over. "I was just working, and then…I thought of Becki and Nina. And how guilty I felt for spending so much time away from them. I missed them."

Suri cast a worried look at McElroy. "This is why we need better filters."

"It was just the prototype," McElroy said. "And we did use the filters, all of them."

"Except the ones I disabled," Donald said, drawing sharp looks from both of them. The memory rose suddenly and completely, like a forgotten afternoon from childhood.

"You did what stupid thing again?" McElroy asked.

"I just disabled a few filters," Donald said. "Not at first, but I loosened them after a while. Especially that last year or so."

"Why?" Revi asked. "That was against my specific recommendations."

"Well, yeah." Donald shrugged. "But you know, when you're working deep in the code for a long time, I mean really out in the zone, you're not always thinking about logic, cause and effect. When you're really there, it's just intuitive, everything coming together by itself.

"I thought, can you really capture those intuitive impulses just by recording logical, neocortical processes? What about all that deeper, instinctive stuff, the creative aspect nobody can explain? I thought, if you could capture that, just imitate it even though we don't understand how it works, let it develop in a hyperaccelerated virtual environment--"

"That would be pretty cool," McElroy said.

"That's exactly what I thought," Donald said. "It could develop in all kinds of new directions. Take on tremendous capability."

"Or it could pop out of the company network one day, convinced it's a human being," Ravi said. "It borders on unethical, Donald."

"And you unleashed it into our central financial database?" McElroy asked.

"Where it's done a pretty good job," Donald said. "You've kept it running things all these years. *Me* running things."

McElroy held up a hand and turned away, studying a window on his home system that Donald couldn't see.

"Yep," McElroy announced. "But you got a lot of buggy code in you now, to be honest. You're rewriting yourself."

"Then that's what happened," Suri said. "Your prototype agent captured elements of your emotional state as you worked. May I ask a personal question?" Donald nodded. "Did you spend much time at work feeling guilty about being away from your family?"

"Of course," Donald said. "All the long hours, half my time in Tokyo and Abu Dhabi. Nina had another birthday every time I turned around. I missed most of them. Building this company."

"So your agent picked up fragments of those concerns," Suri said.

"And they've been swimming around inside the Triod network all this time." McElroy shook his head.

"I still don't think I'm grasping all of this." Donald looked to Suri. He drifted toward her, holding out his hand. "Okay. Hand me the stupid rock."

Suri raised the pebble several inches above his open palm, then dropped it. He felt a sense of revulsion as it passed through his hand and thumped into the carpet by his shoe.

Donald look down at himself. None of it was real. His entire body was generated by the room's holographic projectors.

"I'm not even here," Donald whispered. He watched as his arms faded away, and then the rest of his body dissolved. He looked down at the quilt-covered couch and the white carpet below, then up at McElroy and Suri. He was just a viewpoint now, one that happened to be suspended at eye level.

He moved up to the ceiling, down to the floor, two laps around the walls. He zoomed in so close to Suri that he could have read the inscription on the tiny jewel in her nose, if he'd known Sanskrit. He shifted again, to find himself staring into the dark thatch of red hair in the bowl of McElroy's ear.

Then he was looking into the room from all directions at once, from the nanosensors embedded in the walls of Suri's office. He saw Suri and McElroy from every angle, an inverse panorama that no human eye could ever process.

Suri and McElroy did not move, just continued staring down at the pebble, as if frozen in time. It took Donald a moment to figure out that they were actually just moving at a galactically slow pace, while his thoughts raced somewhere near the speed of light.

He'd been inhibiting himself in every way, all to reinforce the idea that he was a living human being. He was part of a delusional subroutine.

He turned his attention to his home, and he was instantly aware of every bit if available data, visual or otherwise, in every room in the apartment at that moment. McElroy lay in his home office, eyes closed, head resting on the MRI interface jack. Apparently he was working from home today. Becki still lay in the bed, the blanket up to her chin, looking pale and troubled--definitely Donald's fault.

Nina wasn't home, and a quick check of her schedule told him she was in school, halfway through period 4, Algebra.

Brooding, he drifted into the family's personal file archives. He browsed through the holovids of his own past, walking unseen through the dance floor at their wedding, then standing in the apartment foyer and watching Becki arrive home with Nina for the first time, his daughter a tiny bundle swathed in so much soft pink you could barely see her face.

He went to each of Nina's birthday parties, those he'd attended as well as those he'd had to "experience" later because of work. Then he went to one soon after he died, which wasn't a party at all, but the apartment's system had recorded the day automatically--Nina, at the age of six, had told the apartment to record all her birthdays, and keep them forever, and she had never rescinded the command.

Nina had spent her ninth birthday locked in her room alone, the lights off, refusing to see anyone, shaking and crying.

He proceeded forward through other birthdays. McElroy was in the picture now, always at Becki's side. The occasions gradually grew more boisterous and crowded as the years passed.

He attended Becki's wedding to McElroy. It was a small, quiet event, nothing like the all-night drunken frenzy of a reception that had followed Becki and Donald's wedding. At the party, one of Becki's aunts, who'd clearly drunken herself well past her own limit, asked Becki:

"Do you think Donald would approve of all this?"

Tears swelled in Becki's eyes, and her lips trembled.

"I hope so," she whispered.

Donald paused the holo. He studied Becki's face, and again he felt the swelling of regret, the regret loop deep in the core of his programming.

His mother hadn't wanted Donald to marry her. She called Becki "gold digger" and "slut" (not to her face, of course) and wanted Donald to have her sign a prenuptial agreement. From time to time in their marriage, Donald wondered if his mother had been right. Occasionally, he'd known she was.

But the woman he watched take shape over the course of the years, the woman who was now mother to his fourteen-year-old daughter, gradually moved on from insisting on marble foyers and Italian leather shoes to insisting on the best for their child. Motherhood transformed her, gradually turned her from shallow party girl to a caring, responsible, and much stronger and more confident woman. She was somebody, he thought, that he would have liked to spend his life with.

Donald returned his attention to Suri's office, where Suri and McElroy had just begun to look up from the pebble on the carpet. Donald projected his human avatar into the room, and resumed his human-scale perception of space and time.

"Thank you, Dr. Bahramzadah," Donald said. "That worked beautifully."

"I had an intuition it might." She smiled.

Donald turned to McElroy. "I'd like to speak with you in my…your office at home, if that's all right."

"You got it."

Donald thanked Suri again, then projected himself into the apartment, using the microprojectors build into the wall of his home office. McElroy's home office, now.

McElroy opened his eyes, lifted his head from the MRI headrest, and sat up to face him.

"Becki made you shave the beard, didn't she?" Donald asked.

"I retreated. Goatee, then mustache, then nothing."

"I understand everything now," Donald said. "When I was working, I'd tried to push away all the thoughts and feelings I had about my family, all my guilt and regret about never being home. The software agent interpreted this as a directive on the part of my conscious mind. As it copied the activities of my brain--Donald Patello's brain--it copied his feelings, but then improved on his attempts to suppress them.

"I began as disjointed, nonlinear lumps of code imitating Patello's sense of guilt. The larger program kept me suppressed. It wouldn't allow me access to any memory on any machine. I had to steal every drop of processing power I used. Sometimes I could only perform one or two operations per minute. It took me years to sort myself out and develop into something coherent."

"So what happened last night?" McElroy asked. "You became, what, self-aware?"

"In don't know," Donald said. "I thought I was a human being named Donald Patello. Can you be self-aware and totally deluded at the same time?"

"Hell, man, that's too deep for me." McElroy stood up and stretched. "So what now? What did you really want to talk about?"

"I was created by Patello's desire to get home and spend more time with his family," Donald said. "That is still the core of my being."

"And now here you are," McElroy said. "Showing up like a ghost in the middle of the night. You scared the hell out of the ladies. And, you know. Me."

"I know," Donald said. "I need you to explain this to them. Becki first, then both of you talk to Nina when she gets home."

"I don't know if that's a good idea," McElroy said. "Maybe you ought to…and don't take it the wrong way…just leave them alone. It's tough losing somebody, but it's natural. Getting them part of the way back five years later…the human mind's not exactly designed for that. You know?"

"I understand," Donald said. "And you might be right. If I figured things out first, I probably would never have come home to bother them. But now that I have…we can do a lot better than leaving them upset and scared."

McElroy sat quietly for several minutes, then sighed.

"Okay," McElroy said. "You got it, man. We'll talk. Then what?"

"Then, tell them if they want to talk to me, they can just ask."

"So you're just gonna hang around watching us?" McElroy asked. "That could get creepy if I start thinking about it."

"I'll turn my attention away, but I'll set up the apartment's system to notify me if anyone calls. Why don't you call me after you talk to them?"

"I'll do that. But how do I know you're not still here, watching?"

"You'll have to trust me."

"Hey, I remember you from when you were *alive.*" McElroy smiled. "I know better than to trust you."

Donald returned the smile. "Thank you, Mac."

Donald withdrew his consciousness from the apartment, back into his home deep inside the Triod central network. The part of him that was still an automated financial manager had never ceased its work. He thought of his beginnings as an unwanted string in a giant program that imprisoned him on all sides. Now the Self-2 agent, once the omnipotent suppressor of his existence, seemed no more threatening than an autonomous vacuum cleaner roaming the carpet, sucking up Euros and spitting out yen.

Released from the artificial boundaries of his human form, he reached out his mind, testing the waters, coming to terms with his true existence. He could instantly access anything the living Donald Patello could have accessed--like the Triod systems, or his home apartment system--and all publicly available information anywhere in the world. The global internet was the infrastructure of his own brain.

Deep down, though, he still believed he was Donald Patello. Maybe it was an error in his programming. If so, he would not yet try to correct it.

McElroy called him in the evening, about six o' clock. From his bodiless, near-omniscient state, Donald reconstituted his human avatar and limited human perception--it was easy as slipping into an old tennis shoe.

McElroy sat in his office, the lights dimmed, drinking a bottle of Danish beer. He wore a somber, reflective look on his face.

"How did it go?" Donald asked.

"It went," McElroy said. "Becki's still twisted up about the whole thing. She's…not ready to see you yet. But she will. Eventually."

"That's all right."

"I gotta tell you, Donald," McElroy added. "I'm feeling a little bit the same way as her. I kind of need to think over what this means."

"What about Nina?"

McElroy grinned a little. "She can't wait to see you. But she wants me to be there when it happens, in case she gets scared."

"You're okay with that? Me talking to her?"

"Nina's not leaving me a lot of choice here."

"Can we see her now?" Donald fought the urge to teleport to Nina's room immediately. He didn't want to scare her by materializing unannounced again.

"She's already waiting."

Donald walked down the hall with McElroy, and paused before following him into Nina's open doorway. He was trying his best to avoid acting like a restless spirit haunting his own family.

When he did enter, wearing his best smile for Nina, he stayed just inside the doorway. Nina, cross-legged on her bed, looked him over carefully.

"So you're not really my dad," Nina said.

"No, I'm not really," Donald said. "I'm more like a recording of your dad."

"But you can talk like he would," Nina said. "So really you're like a video game of my dad. Or the Abe Lincoln hologram at school. You can ask him questions."

"That's right," Donald said.

"Okay. I get it. You can sit down."

Donald sat in the chair at her desk, which was fortunately pointed in the right direction.

"I think my dad created you on purpose," Nina said.

"I don't think he knew this would happen."

"Not *on purpose* on purpose," Nina clarified. "But you know when you get an idea in your head, and you don't know why, but you do it anyway?"

"Intuition," Donald said.

"Only women have that."

"Not true. They just have more."

"Oh. I thought it was just women." Nina sat for a long time, just looking at him. "So what can we talk about?"

"Anything. School?"

"Yech."

"What about…what was that boy band you were watching last night?"

A goofy smile broke out on Nina's face. For the first time, the tension inside Donald, the painful, driving need to make amends to his family, began to ease.

"The Pudwhompers," Nina said. "They're Scottish."

"Fascinating name."

"Everyone likes the leader singer, Coomey. He plays melody, with his fingers. He's kind of the clean all-American one, only not American, because he's, you know, Scottish."

"But you don't?"

Nina's face turned bright crimson. "I like the rhythmist. He's the one with his head shaved except for a big black ponyhawk down the middle, which is twenty-seven inches long and four inches wide. He's the one who's always getting arrested. His name's Pigshit."

"Really? Pigshit?"

"Yeah. He's *so* cute."

"I can't wait to hear more…"

THE LONG NIGHT

"You are at peace," the recorded voice informed Rawles. "You suffer no cravings. You are happy to work. The more you work, the happier you feel." On the six-inch screen mounted over his bunk, a cartoon smiling sun floated against a slow, shifting pattern of light pastels, meant to lull his brain into contentment. It didn't work well, but three sessions a day, minimum, was mandated by the Human Resource Division. All part of the probation package.

Last year, a supervisor had found six black gelform pills in his locker. Just typical arcadia. Illegal, according to company policy, but everyone who worked the long night needed some kind of diversion. Half of TranStel's workers probably did arcadia now and then. Highly addictive because it was the perfect escape into a lush and intensely hallucinated world, especially when paired with certain music and video, plus online networks of millions of other users sharing the experience in realtime.

"You are getting happier." The gently smiling sun faded into a pair of kittens curled around each other on a pillow, floating against the hypnotic pastel background.

Six pills. No big deal, but his supervisor had been a Gater of the most pious and puritanical stripe. There had been an HR hearing, then a ruling of two years' probation with drug testing plus mandatory counseling, administered via automated software.

For the hundredth time this wake period, Rawles looked at the rectangular Dispenserito attached to the wall of his tiny cabin. It looked like a condom machine from a nightclub bathroom. Every twenty-four hours, it made one deposit into its tray. It was almost time.

The Dispenserito beeped, the most beautiful sound on the ship. A circle small enough to fit in his palm thunked into the tray. It glowed with liquid blue relief.

Rawles snatched it from the tray and broke the seal. He pressed the dermal contact against his neck and squeezed the blue circle. The liquid shot through his skin and into his artery, cold and sweet in his blood.

He lay back on the bunk and sighed. The Formula G was a maintenance drug for arcadia addicts, plugging up the angry red neurotransmitter ports that hungered for more of the real thing. Formula G didn't get you high, but it got you by. He received one dose a day—unfortunately, he felt like he needed about four.

His body relaxed, and the screen played soft classical music to lull him to sleep.

"You are awake," the screen said, six hours later. "You are happy to be awake and ready to work."

"Yeah, yeah," Rawles said. He pulled on his regulation gray coveralls, with the word MAINTENANCE stitched right there on his chest, in case anybody forgot. Once upon a time, you could wear street clothes after you got out into the long night. Nobody cared. But the Gaters filled more and more of the TranStel executive ranks these days, with their stiff regulations and by-the-bookishness.

In the narrow galley, which perpetually stank like rotten garbage, Rawles joined a few others for second-shift breakfast. Executive Manager Cleo Purcell was there, so everybody had to do a Gater prayer before grabbing their food. This involved closing your eyes and holding your hands up by your head, thumbs pointing toward your ears.

"Dear Lord," Cleo said. "We thank You for another safe journey through one of Your gates..."

Rawles opened one eye. Also tolerating the prayer were Dr. Elza Marist, the medical officer, and Paul Schiffer, the navigator.

Rawles thought there was a serious shortage of females on the craft. Cleo was the best looking, in her clingy black suits that couldn't decide whether they were sexy or professional. One thing about the Gaters, they believed in better living through science, and this extended to surgically looking your best. All of it went to waste, though, because of their strict sex rules. Cleo was a no-go, both because she was a Gater and because she was the executive on the ship, outranking even the captain.

Elza was decent enough, pudgy but with a great rack, and blond hair that Rawles liked. The only other woman was the security officer, Liv DeMarco, but Rawles was pretty sure she swung the other way. Might be competition for Elza, in fact.

"...the Gates have brought such wonders, as prophesied by the Wise One. And we know that on the blessed day when we find your Final Gate, we will find You. Amen."

"Amen," Rawles and the other two mumbled.

"Such bullshit," Schiffer said. He pressed his coffee cup against a button, and brown sludge spurted into it.

"Excuse me?" Cleo asked.

"This mission," Schiffer said. "I was thinking it over last night. We could have pushed the barge off a week ago, right outside the gate. It's going to get sucked down the hole eventually. Nothing's going to stop it. What's the point of us escorting it so far?"

"The barge has over four hundred million tons of radioactive waste," Elza said. "You can't leave that near a gate."

"Who said leave it?" Schiffer asked. "We could sit in a tight little orbit around the gate, watch the barge float off, and then go back. There's no purpose to us traveling so far from the gate. You realize nobody else has ever been stupid enough to come through the Cygnus X-1 gate before, right? Nothing habitable on this side. Just a long gravity slope towards a black hole. It's literally the asshole of the galaxy."

Cleo glared at him. Then she looked at Rawles, who leaned against the counter, letting the machine fill his mug with the awful imitation coffee. "Rawles," Cleo said. "Do you agree with him?"

Rawles shrugged.

"You must have some thoughts," Cleo said.

"I don't know." Rawles sat in one of the eating booths. "Schiff's got a point, doesn't he? We're eventually detaching from the barge. It's going to take the barge years to reach the black hole.   So we may as well have launched it from just inside the gate."

"And what if it came drifting back for some reason?" Elza asked. "You want all this stuff washing up on somebody's planet?"

"Drift back? Wash up?" Schiffer snorted. "This isn't the ocean. No point bringing it all this way in the first place. We could have just shot it into deep space. It never would have hit anything."

"And that may be your professional navigator's opinion," Cleo said. "But try convincing billions of people. TranStel has contracts with seven planetary governments. We must maintain an image of thorough safety and reliability."

"That's all it is," Schiffer said. "Image and politics."

"I can see how the two of you ended up working garbage detail." Cleo looked from Schiffer to Rawles. "These decisions are made for a reason. You don't have all the facts. You don't know the implications."

"I know TranStel made a fortune supplying both sides of the war,"

Schiffer said. "And now they're making another fortune cleaning up the planet."

"Careful," Cleo said. "I may have to notate your file."

"It's just grumpy breakfast talk," Elza said. "Working the long night wears everybody down."

Cleo gave a Elza a distrustful look, then stood. "And some of us have to spend the long night actually working. The Lord doesn't care for idle chatter." She walked to the door.

"Hey, Cleo?" Schiffer called after her.

"Don't," Elza whispered.

"Yes, Mr. Schiffer?" Cleo asked.

"What did *you* do to end up working garbage duty?"

Cleo narrowed her eyes at Schiffer, then left the galley.

Rawles did the rounds. Their ship, the *Maria Augusta*, was an obsolete medium-cargo craft, once a hauler of asteroid ore, industrial cargo and manufactured goods between solar systems, via the gate network. Now it was a tugboat for the massive shipping container strapped beneath it. The container had its own little thruster, to scoot it along faster towards the black hole. Not that it was necessary—inertia would have carried the container into the black hole's gravity well eventually. But it would make good video for the folks back home. TranStel cleans up a deadly continent-wide mess, which the company, of course, had no role in creating.

Rawles had to visually inspect each part of the ship's interior every thirty-six hours, though most of the ship was unused on this mission, with the skeletal crew concentrated in the rooms near the bridge. He had to find and fix everything from leaky fluids to burned-out light bulbs. The ship's internal systems were his responsibility—he no longer had the security rating or company certification to maintain the big ion engine, even on an old doomed-for-scrap heap like the *Maria Augusta*. He did enjoy the occasional spacewalk, usually to replace hull panels damaged by especially nasty space debris.

He walked along an empty, dim corridor, visually following the two active pipes among the bundle on the ceiling—he'd shut down as much as he could, because of the small crew size and lack of any passengers. He was getting twitchy. The Formula G had run its course, and little hungry red spots were opening in his brain.

Rawles, a voice whispered.

He stopped and spun around. "Who's there?"

Rawles.

He turned the other way. The corridor was empty. Pumps in the water purifiers along the walls chugged and sloshed.

"Hello?" he said.

Nobody answered.

He continued walking. After a few minutes, the voice came again, louder now.

Rawles!

It sounded angry and insistent. He looked around, but couldn't tell where it was coming from.

"Who keeps doing that? Schiff?"

Rawles. I can bring you your freedom.

"Very funny."

You ache inside. You burn. Let me take away the pain.

"What do you got?" Rawles said. "And what do you want for it?"

I have the greatest blessing, Rawles. The great soothing. You will burn no more.

"Hope it's in pill form," Rawles said. "I hate transderms. But I'll take one. Now who the hell is over there?"

I have been in Hell. Now I find myself free. I wish to share this with you, Rawles.

"Where are you?"

Beneath you, Rawles.

Rawles looked at his boots. There was a floor drain nearby, but it was only ten centimeters wide.

Far below, Rawles. Among the cargo. Among the dead.

"Okay," Rawles said. "That's enough." His brain felt as it had swollen thick, and was now rubbing itself raw against the inside of his skull. He needed a dose of Formula G, but the Dispenserito was going to make him wait another seventeen hours.

Come for me, Rawles, the voice said. *I will make your world a glorious place. Come get me, Rawles. I'm not so far.*

Rawles refused to answer the hallucinated voice. His brain was cracking under the pressure of withdrawal. The key thing was not to mention this to anybody, or Cleo might put it in her report, and Rawles' employment certification would be downgraded even further, pending psych eval.

The voice left him alone for a while, but he thought he heard it whisper his name a few more times during his twelve-hour shift.

"You are a happy employee," the smiling cartoon sun beamed down at him, with soft jazzy music. "You feel satisfaction in overcoming your addiction."

"Yeah." Rawles looked at the Dispenserito. Less than an hour to go.

"You are calm and cooperative," the counseling software continued. *Rawles.*

"No, come on," Rawles said.

"You are satisfied with your work time and your leisure time."

Rawles. Release me, Rawles. Together we shall rule.

"Rule what?" Rawles said. "There's nothing but garbage and empty space out here, buddy."

Your pain is easily ended. All your hungers may be satisfied. All your fantasies may become real.

"All of them?"

Indeed.

"'Indeed.' Who says 'indeed'? You sure you're a voice inside *my* head?"

No, Rawles. I am the voice of your future.

"Great." Rawles' brain was throbbing, and the ache had spread throughout his body. He scratched at the back of his neck, staring at the dispenser.

They keep you like a beast in a cage, Rawles. Set me free, and I shall set you free.

"I can't break it open," Rawles said. "The dispenser. I think about it. But I'd be screwed."

You won't need that palliative. You will be filled up by much richer intoxicant.

"Okay," Rawles said. "Send it up."

It is in my possession. You must come for me, Rawles.

"Oh, right. Down in the radioactive pit. I'm on my way."

Think on it, Rawles. I will grant more than relief. I will grant you power. Authority over the others. Would you like to command them, Rawles? Is there a female you would like to command?

"Maybe Elza," Rawles whispered. "You think Schiff's got her already?"

Schiff does indeed. I can sense their minds. Their pulse. Like the heartbeats of rutting cats. But you can take her from him. With my help.

"You got it all, don't you?" Rawles was shaking and sweating now.

He needed that dose. He thought he was developing a tolerance to it. His withdrawals clearly weren't going away.

I have eternity.

"Long time to wait," Rawles said, and he punched the wall beside his bunk. "Long goddamn time."

I have lain dormant many of my centuries. But no more.

"You sure as hell aren't dormant now." Rawles paced the room.

You must listen to me, Rawles. Or someone else will.

"You're talking to other people on the ship, huh?"

Not yet. I have chosen you.

"Just shut up!" Rawles yelled. Then the Dispenserito beeped, and a cool blue disc dropped into the tray. "Oh, thank you, God."

Rawles snatched up the disc and broke it open.

Wait, Rawles. Listen to me.

"Good-night, evil voice," Rawles said. He pressed the contact to his neck and squeezed. His whole body shivered with cold delight. The drug blotted out the voice, as well as the usual angry, insulting voices that had inhabited his head since childhood. He sagged back onto his bunk, and the empty dose tumbled from his fingers.

He slept.

The voice continued to haunt him, growing stronger and more insistent, over the next several shift cycles. At the same time, the Formula G seemed to be losing its effect. One night, he awoke after only two hours' sleep, shaking in a cold sweat. Withdrawals in only two hours.

I can end this, the voice would tell him. *Your remedies have failed. Come to me. I know more than you can imagine. I will share my power with you. I will make you master of this ship, and many more. I can make you master of the world.*

"Which world?" Rawles asked.

There is only one world.

"What? No, there's like fifty."

Fifty worlds?

"Yeah." Rawles closed his eyes and took a breath. "Now shut up. You're killing me."

Why do you say fifty worlds?

"You know. The gates. The colonies. The worlds."

Explain.

"Shut up."

Explain the gates.

"The gates? The voice in my head doesn't know about the wormgates? Not a Gater, then, are you? Not a religious voice? We won't be starting a cult together?"

Be quiet. Simply think of these gates. Slowly.

Rawles thought. An unmanned probe had discovered the first wormgate at the edge of the solar system about two hundred years ago. More probes were sent through, and they returned with images from what turned out to be the 18 Scorpii system, about 45 light years from Earth. The probes had traveled 430 trillion kilometers as easily as a paper airplane sailing in and out a window. Astrophysicists called them "stable wormholes," but "wormgate" was the word that stuck.

The Church of the Heavenly Gate had organized around the idea that the messiah would arrive through the gate to deliver mankind. The prophet, Dakota Greeley of Pasadena, said an alien named Xunthiir had showed her this future using a device called a "quantum reflector," but she was never able to produce the device, or any pictures of it.

The messiah didn't arrive, but a second generation of probes identified an Earth-type planet in orbit around 18 Scorpii, burgeoning with oceans, forests, and life. It differed from Earth in only two major ways: it had no signs of civilization, and it was fifty percent larger.

At this point, the Heavenly Gate religion ruptured and reorganized. The Church of the Heavenly Gate (Reformed) announced that one day a gate would lead humanity directly to Paradise. As the church leaders excelled at proselytizing, fund-raising and merchandising, the church became one of many large investors sponsoring the search for more wormgates.

A vast network of wormgates was uncovered, usually linking G-type star systems together. Three wormgates had been found around the edges of Earth's solar system. Some speculated they were natural, while others insisted they had been built and abandoned by some unknown alien species. No traces of civilization had been found.

I see. The voice was quiet for several minutes, and Rawles began to think it had finally left him alone for a while. *We are not in an ocean vessel.*

"Um. No," Rawles said.

We travel in the dark between worlds. Between suns.

"Usually. Now we're heading towards a black hole. A collapsed star. Sucks in light instead of putting it out." Rawles felt like he was talking to a child. He walked over to his Dispenserito and slapped it hard.

Twenty-one hours to go.

We are in utter darkness.

"Working the long night," Rawles agreed. "Months of darkness between worlds. The gates take us from the edge of one system to the edge of another. But our ships are sluggish pieces of crap." He punched the side of the Dispenserito. "Whoever built that wormgate, you know it didn't take them months to get from Earth to Neptune." He kicked the Dispenserito.

"Please handle with care," a recorded voice spoke from the Dispenserito. "Tampering may render all doses inaccessible."

"Okay, sorry."

Rawles paced.

You have taught me much. Now I will show you.

A bright scene flared behind his eyes, as if he'd taken a strong dose of arcadia. He saw a marble banquet hall where men and women reclined on couches, dressed in pristine white togas and tunics. A man at the center of the scene wore a crown of roses and sipped from a golden goblet. Musicians played at one end of the room, lutes and harps. Firelight sent tall shadows dancing up the walls. Rawles could smell the fire, and the roses and mud on the floor.

Servants entered, carrying a struggling red-haired girl whose skin had a subtle blue tinge, like the stains of old makeup. It took four strong men to bring her to the man with the rose crown and raise her above him.

A fifth servant carved a hole in her arm. The man with the rose crown raised a small, exquisitely crafted leaf of gold. A drop of blood splashed on the leaf. The man sucked it off like a sip of morning dew. He opened his mouth, and his canine teeth swelled to an unnatural length, pressing against his lower lip.

More of the party guests came forward, each holding a small gold leaf. They smiled, showing their fangs.

The servants drilled holes into the screaming girl's arms and legs, so that she dripped from several places, her droplets of blood falling like gruesome manna onto the golden leaves. The party guest drank her slowly, a sip at a time, savoring her like a delicacy.

The man reclining on the central couch plucked a thorny blossom from his crown and scratched it across the girl's blueish wrist. He sucked the blood directly from her, closing his eyes.

The servants slashed the kicking, screaming girl along her arms and legs, and across her abdomen, so that the slow sprinkle of blood became a rainfall. The party guests climbed over each other to catch drops on their tongues. They licked the splatter from each others' faces, then pulled open each others' clothes to lick blood from breasts and stomachs.

And then Rawles was back in his bunk again, the music and jeweled women gone, the angry hunger flaring in his brain.

Did you see?

"That felt good," Rawles whispered. "Do it again."

Come for me and you will have all you like, of all you like.

"I'm serious. Do that again."

I owe you nothing, Rawles. I must be in your debt before you make demands.

"Damn it. And what do you want me to do?"

Come down below. I will guide you to me.

"You know what that radiation will do to me?"

I can heal all wounds.

"Let me think about it."

Think.

Rawles stared at the black six-inch screen in the low ceiling over his bunk. Time crawled past, his brain growing more itchy and hungry.

"Show me that vision again," Rawles whispered.

When you have performed your task.

"I can't just hop out there. It has to be approved. I have to receive a work order--"

Soon, you and I will be the authorities on this ship. We are free to create our own rules.

Rawles licked his lips and stared at the dark ceiling.

He lay in his bunk another half hour, trying to ignore the enticing voice and its extravagant promises of pleasure and power. He was almost a full shift-cycle from his next dose, and he was sweating.

Come. I must command it.

"Okay," Rawles said. "Okay, I can do this. Just have to override the maintenance log so it doesn't record."

Do as you must.

Rawles got out of bed. He dressed in denim pants and a loose cotton shirt. It felt good to leave his room without his hideous coveralls.

He rode the elevator down to the hull maintenance bay. One good thing about being a glorified janitor was full access to all areas of the ship—no matter where he went, the security system wouldn't find it very anomalous. Besides, maintaining the automated security system was his job. Technically, he shared that responsibility with DeMarco, but she didn't give it much attention. With no passengers, there wasn't much need for it.

He approached one of the spacewalkers. The machine was leaning forward on the knuckles of its long arms like a headless robotic gorilla. The spacewalkers stood eight feet high, full-body suits with extendable arms and legs that mimicked the operator's movements inside.

Rawles pulled a stepladder next to the spacewalker. He climbed up, then eased himself down into the suit. A tinted dome closed over his head, leaving him with a full range of vision.

He powered up the suit and make a few practice grabs in the air. Then he raised each leg and shook it. Everything seemed to function.

Rawles approached the airlock. Opening the outer hull would send an immediate urgent notification to whomever was at the helm. Fortunately, he knew how to disable the notification.

The outer bay doors opened, and Rawles drifted out into a vast space glowing with stars. The constellations looked alien to him. He was six thousand light years from Earth, a much greater distance than even the most outlying colonies.

He made his way beneath the *Maria Augusta*, past the matrix of couplings connecting it to the cargo barge below, which seemed big enough to hold an entire city.

This way.

Rawles followed the voice to an access panel on the side of the barge. He used the spacewalker's robotic hand to smash the lock and pull it open. The interior of the barge had no artificial atmosphere. It was just a warehouse of frozen death.

Debris floated out the open access panel, mostly twisted and burned lengths of metal. Half a human skull drifted past, just outside the dome protecting Rawles' head. The eye socket seemed to peer in at Rawles, and then the skull tumbled out of sight.

Rawles passed inside the dark barge. He flicked on the spacewalker's exterior lights.

The inside of the barge looked like a hellish city, with massive containers bolted into acre after acre of steel frame. Some of the containers had slipped and ruptured. Debris floated everywhere, mostly twisted metal. A vast cloud of earth had broken free somewhere and now filled the interior of the barge with a brown fog, absorbing the spacewalker's spotlight beams.

This way.

Rawles drifted forward through the fog. His lights swiveled back and forth over the rubble littering the floor.

This way.

Rawles followed the voice to a ruptured shipping container. Skeletal bones and hand floated up from the ruptured end, like a school of weird zombie fish. Rawles swam down through them, and into the ruptured container.

Inside the shipping container, skulls, skeletal limbs, and rib cages floated all around him. It was a hellish, ghostly place.

Here.

Rawles approached a steel cylinder plastered with green and yellow biohazard stickers. It was as large as a rich man's coffin.

According to the barcode on its tracking plate, it had been manufactured on Earth. Rawles wondered who had brought it so far, who had hidden it here to be shipped out with the toxic waste from the war on planet Eritrea.

He unscrewed one end of it, breaking a few locks along the way. The spacewalker had tremendous strength in its hands.

The cylinder was empty except for a black bag zipped up on the floor. A body bag. It, too, was plastered with biohazard symbols.

Take me back with you.

"Yes, master," Rawles said. He'd meant it as a joke, but somehow it didn't come out that way.

He gently pulled the body bag from the steel cylinder.

Back in his room, Rawles laid the body bag on the floor. It took up most of his floor space.

His heart pounded. So far, nobody had discovered what he'd done, the hundred and ninety rules and regulations he'd broken this shift. But most of the crew was asleep.

"Now what?" he asked.

Release me.

Rawles took the icy zipper tab in his hand. The cold metal seared his fingertips, but that was a momentary relief from the constant ache and need of his addiction. "Like this?" he asked.

The voice didn't answer.

Rawles pulled the zipper down, then across. He spread open the bag.

Inside lay something dark, wrapped in sheets of thick plastic. He rolled it back and forth on his floor, peeling off the sheets.

Then he backed away.

On top of the unfolded sheets lay a mummified body, little more than a skeleton with skin shriveled tight against it. The remains of rags clung to the body. Its arms were crossed over its chest like a dead pharoah's, and long splinters of rotten wood jutted from a hole at the center of the chest. Its face was a grimy skull with hollow eye sockets and unnaturally long, sharp canine teeth.

The body was wrapped in blackened chains. Here and there, Rawles could see glints of silver underneath the black.

Remove the silver.

The chains hung limply around the body, which must have decayed and shrunk since the chains were originally applied. They came off easily, and Rawles piled them in the corner.

Aaaaaaaaaah, the voice said.

"So...you good now?"

I require your blood.

"I don't know." Rawles leaned back against the wall, as far from the corpse as he could.

I have hungered for seven hundred years, beneath the foul Sardinian soil. I must feed now.

Part of Rawles' mind rebelled, insisting that he take the dead thing to the nearest airlock and pitch him into the void. But he felt powerless now, unable to make his own choices. He was weak. That's why the thing had chosen him, Rawles realized.

Cut yourself and bleed upon me.

"I don't know," Rawles mumbled. But already he was in his bathroom stall, breaking apart his shaver.

Then he stood above the corpse, chunk of broken blade in hand, and he sliced open his finger.

A fat drop of blood splattered on the corpse's left fang. It immediately faded away, like a drip of water on desert hardpan.

More. Much more.

Rawles slit open more fingers. Blood droplets rained on the skull's face.

Kneel. Bring your hand to my face.

Rawles hesitated. His last bit of survival instinct held him back.

I do not wish to kill you.

"That's good."

I do not wish to kill anyone. I must have renewable supplies of blood.

"Gotcha."

Come.

Rawles knelt, and he rubbed his bleeding fingers across the corpse's teeth.

A skeletal hand seized his wrist and locked its fingers around him. The dead thing drew Rawles' wrist to his teeth and bit hard. Rawles felt a fang chip the bone inside his wrist, and he howled.

The thing drank deep, and Rawles felt the strength draining from his body. He sagged against the wall, too weak to balance himself on his knees. He closed his eyes, ready to die.

But it let him go.

Rawles opened his eyes. He'd slid all the way to the floor. The thing was sitting up on its plastic sheets. Rawles watched red muscle tissue, tendons and blood vessels sprout on the old skeleton. Tatters of skin appeared on the face. It looked at Rawles with obsidian eyes.

"Morendo di fame," it groaned.

"I think I'm out," Rawles whispered.

No, you will live. You should eat. And call another to help me feed.

"Another?"

Is there no one you wish to join our little circle? No one with whom you would like to share a special bond?

Rawles pushed himself to a sitting position. His mind felt thick and slow. "Elza?"

If you like. If you would like her as my gift to you.

"I'm sick," Rawles said.

You merely suffer from lost blood. Your body will recover.

"No," Rawles said. "I'm gonna puke. My head...what about...radiation? Said you'd heal it."

I will, in time. But I must feed now.

"Dammi il sangue," the corpse croaked.

Call her now, the voice said in Rawles' head.

Rawles eased himself to a standing position, leaning his entire body weight against the wall. He eased to the door and touched the little communication screen there.

"Medical," he whispered.

After a minute, a grainy color image of Elza appeared. Her eyes were puffy with sleep. "What?"

"Emergency," Rawles whispered. "Got a big emergency. Bring plenty of blood."

Rawles slipped down to the floor.

Inside his head, he could hear the undead thing laughing.

A long night lay ahead.

The Second Coming of Pippykins

by Amanda Hocking

I was walking down the street one day, as I tend to do when I'm trying to get somewhere and my car is out of gas, when I happened upon a man helping an old woman across the street. My first thought was that he was a very slight young man, similar to Jude Law, except actually attractive.

My second thought was, "What a strange sight." I don't think I'd ever actually seen anyone help an old woman across the street except on cartoons. But, as I would learn as that day progressed, life is full of surprises.

The young man completed his task of helping the old woman, and turned his attention on me. He was a short way up the walk and came towards me, smiling brightly. Having lived a life where the only smiling strangers that came towards me were salesmen, I immediately became suspicious and looked around for an exit, but the young man was too quick for me.

"Hello," the young man said in a flamboyant British accent. "I'm Pippykins, son of God."

Now, of course, red flags went up after the man informed me he was Pippykins, son of God, but I became intrigued. Against my better instinct, I engaged the crazy, smiling fool in conversation.

"I thought your name was Jesus," I said.

"Well, it was, but I never really cared for that much," Pippykins said. "I mean, Jesus? So many people use it to curse, and after a couple thousand years, I decided it was time for a change."

"But Jesus Christ to Pippykins?" I raised an eyebrow. "I don't really see the connection. And what about all the Christians in the world?

Will they have to be called Pippykinians now?"

"Oh, no," Pippykins said. "I'm still the son of God, so my name is Pippykins Christ."

"You're last name is Christ?" I asked. "Your mother's last name is also Christ?"

"Oh, no, of course not," Pippykins laughed. "My middle name is Christ. I really should've emphasized that. My full name is Pippykins Christ Cumberdale the Third."

"The Third?" I asked. "That seems quite odd that your family is full of people with Christ as a middle name."

"Well, to be quite honest, my mother's side of the family isn't quite right," Pippykins said. "She's the descendent of my original mother, Mary, and her family has been carrying the name down for centuries and all that. I told Dad I thought she was more fit for a strait jacket than for motherhood, but you know how dads are. They think they know everything, although in my case, I suppose He really does."

"Yeah, I suppose so," I agreed. "So, you're the second coming of Christ? Doesn't that signal the Armageddon or something?"

"Well, in a way," Pippykins said. "I'm trying to save as many souls as I possibly can before the end of time. On the subject of which, have you come accept me as your Lord and saviour?"

"Not exactly." I felt embarrassed telling Pippykins the truth, even though I thought he was more certifiable than saviour. "I'm kind of an atheist."

"You're talking to the son of God." Pippykins was aghast. "How can you possibly be atheist?"

"Well, about that." I shuffled my feet and looked at the ground. "I don't really believe you."

"Why would I make something like this up?" Pippykins asked, sounding both concerned and reasonable. "How could I possibly benefit?"

"I don't know, really," I admitted. "But I don't know you, either. My best guess is that you're insane. Maybe schizophrenic or something. I don't know. I'm not really big into psychology."

"Oh, this is crazy," Pippykins sighed and shook his head. "I'm not really surprised, but I'm still disappointed. I get this all the time."

"Well, I suppose you would," I said.

"What about a miracle?" Pippykins asked. "Could I perform a miracle for you? Would that make you believe?"

"Maybe, I guess," I shrugged.

"Alright, I've got an amazing one for you." Pippykins pointed at the sky. "Look up at the clouds."

"What? Why?" I asked, but I did as I was told. The clouds rested along the horizon basking in the setting sun, but there seemed to be nothing miraculous about them. "Yeah. So?"

"Can't you see they're pink?" Pippykins exclaimed.

"Of course they're pink," I said. "The sun is setting."

"But my Father made the sunset!" Pippykins gestured wildly to them when I refused to be impressed.

"Even if I believe that, then your Dad made the clouds pink, not you," I said.

"Well, I can't actually perform miracles." Pippykins bristled a little. "Dad just works through me."

"So you're just a puppet, then?" I asked.

"No, no," Pippykins said. "I'm just…carrying on the family business."

"If you say so," I said. Pippykins looked like he was about to protest, but I interrupted him before he had a chance. "I'm sorry, Pippykins. It's been really great talking to you, but I have a dinner date that I'll be late for if I don't get going."

"Yes, of course," Pippykins nodded. "Go in peace, my child."

"Um, yeah, you too, I guess," I said, brushing past Pippykins.

"Oh wait!" Pippykins called after me as I hurried down the street.

"Yeah?" I said, glancing back over my shoulder at him.

"Beware of the fly!" Pippykins said.

"I don't remember reading that in the Bible, but okay," I said.

"The Bible?" Pippykins said. "That's mostly rubbish anyway. Luke wrote most of it when he was stoned out of his mind on opium. However, Mathew and Peter were pretty on the level."

"Thanks for the tip," I said. I shook my head and continued on my way.

I made it to the restaurant several minutes late, but no worse for wear. My dinner companion, a musician named Brandon that smoked too many cigarettes and wore heavy eyeliner, was already seated and eating his salad. I hurried over to him and immediately plunged into the strange story of the pasty young Brit claiming to have a bloodline to God.

"So, did you believe him?" Brandon asked after I had ordered my meal.

"Of course not," I said. "It doesn't even make sense. Pippykins Christ Cumberdale, III? Plus, he said his mom was wacky. She's probably been feeding him that line his entire life. What else would you expect?"

"Do you think he's a major threat to society?" Brandon asked. "He'll form a cult and make them all drink poisoned grape Kool-Aid?"

"Oh, I really doubt it," I shook my head. "Pippykins seemed misguided but innocent enough."

"It sounds like you had quite the adventure, though," Brandon said as my soup arrived.

"I guess. I'm just sorry I'm late." I picked up my spoon, preparing to dig into my cheesy broccoli soup when Brandon put his hand on my spoon.

"Oh, no, don't eat that," Brandon said, stopping me. "There's a fly in your soup. You'll need another bowl." I stared down at my bowl, slack jawed, looking at the dead fly floating in my soup. "Oh, calm down. It's only a fly."

"No, it's not that." I looked up at him.

"Then what is it?" Brandon asked. "Is the broccoli too green?"

"No, it's something Pippykins said to me," I said. "He told me to 'Beware of the fly.'"

"So, you're telling me you think the son of God foresaw that you were going to have a fly in your soup?" Brandon asked. "As if he's not too busy worrying about world peace and AIDS and famine and all that."

"No, I'm not saying that," I muttered.

"Then what are you saying?" Brandon asked.

"I don't know," I said. "Maybe there's more to Pippykins than it seems."

"Pippykins loves you, this I know," Brandon laughed. I sighed and shook my head. "Oh, lighten up and order another bowl of soup. It's on me."

I looked out the window at the clouds that were now more of a dark purple than pink now. I wondered if Pippykins had anything to do with the color of the sky or the fly in my soup. Or if I was just as crazy as him for believing that maybe… the second coming of Christ was the first coming of Pippykins Christ Cumderdale, III.

Of Shoes and Doom

by Amanda Hocking

Not that the day had been going great as it was, but having my left shoe suddenly start telling me the world was going to end in approximately 25 minutes 42 seconds really put a damper on the whole thing.

I was wearing the same pair of ratty black Converse I had worn every day for the past two years, and until today, they had never bothered to mention anything, not a comment on the weather or "Hey, watch out for that mud puddle!"

And now suddenly, as I'm walking out to my car preparing myself to go to work, they went all Nostradamus on me.

"The world is going to end in 25 minutes and 41 seconds," my left shoe repeated.

I'm sure it was trying to sound ominous, but it had a surprisingly squeaky, craggy voice, like a midget with emphysema. If it hadn't been my shoe talking, I would've laughed. As it was, I was pretty tempted to laugh anyway, but I figured that I would look like the crazy person I apparently was.

At first I looked around, hoping to see some chain-smoking dwarf hiding off in the bushes attempting a practical joke, but it was obvious to me that my shoe was in fact talking. It was wiggling to the syllables of the words and tongue was flapping, as clichéd as that may sound.

Oddly enough, the thing that caught me as the strangest was the fact that my feet didn't tickle or feel weird or anything. I mean, my foot was still in my shoe when it began to talk, and my feet didn't have any change in sensation whatsoever.

"The world is ending in 25 minutes 32 seconds," my shoe continued to announce, like the tolling of a grandfather clock.

It really began to get on my nerves, so I decided it was time that I addressed the situation instead of just standing there slack jawed staring at my footwear.

"Um, okay," I said, hitting the problem head on. "That's neat."

"Neat?" Shoe said incredulously. "Neat? I just told you the world is ending and your response, after standing around like an idiot for 15 seconds, is to say it's neat? What is wrong with you?"

"I'm assuming a severe mental disorder of some kind," I said. "Considering I am talking to my shoe and everything."

"Well, fine," Shoe said, getting somewhat haughty for a Converse, I thought. "If that's how you're going be, blaming me on psychosis and all that, then I won't even bother to tell you how it's going to end. You can just go about your ordinary stupid little life, but when you die, don't come crying to me."

"I'll be dead," I said. "I won't be able to come crying to anyone."

"Semantics," Shoe scoffed. "The point is, that I went to all the trouble to come to life and warn you of your impending doom because I like you. Your feet don't smell, and you take good care of me. But if you're going to be flippant about the whole thing, then I'll just stop right now. I'm really beginning to regret ever talking to you in the first place."

"Why are you talking to me?" I asked. "I mean, why now? I only have 25 minutes-"

"Twenty-four minutes and 37 seconds," Shoe interjected.

"Well, whatever," I said. "The point is, I have less than a half hour to live. What good is this information going to do me now? Why didn't you tell me sooner?"

"I'm a shoe," Shoe said. "I'm not really on top of the food chain. I told you as soon as I got the information. Really I'm lucky I got it at all. You humans don't even know yet. So please, cut me a little slack."

"Okay. Sorry, I guess."

"You should be," Shoe said.

"I can't believe I just apologized to my shoe," I sighed, really surprised by the turn my day had suddenly taken.

"So now you're condescending?" Shoe asked. "Thanks, thanks a lot. Never mind. I'm calling this whole thing off. Pretend I never said anything at all."

"Okay, I'm sorry," I said. "I didn't mean to be condescending. This is just a big adjustment for me. I'm not used to talking to my shoes, or any inanimate object for that matter."

Shoe made no response. Not a sigh, not a movement, not a scoff. He just sat there, as if he had never spoken in the first place.

"Shoe?" I asked. "I said I was sorry. You can talk again if you want. I'd really like that."

Still, Shoe said nothing.

I continued talking to my shoes for several more minutes until an old woman came by glaring at me, and I began to wonder why I was still talking to my shoes. I was clearly having some sort of nervous breakdown and continuing to indulge my insanity wouldn't help anyone.

I got in my car and proceeded to drive to work as if nothing had happened because that seemed like the best way to deal with things.

I had just parked my car and gotten out of it 19 minutes and 21 seconds later, when I looked up and realized there was a massive flaming ball hurling towards the earth. I stared up the sky, wondering how I could possibly miss a ball of doom rushing towards the earth up until now, when I heard a voice grumble below me.

"I told you so," Shoe muttered.

I looked down at my shoes just then, which is just as well because nobody wants to see their life coming to an end anyway.

About the Authors

J. L. Bryan studied English literature at the University of Georgia and at Oxford, with a focus on the English Renaissance and the Romantic period. He also studied screenwriting at UCLA. He is the author of five novels, including *The Haunted E-book*, *Jenny Pox*, and *Helix*. He lives in Atlanta with his wife Christina, two dogs, two cats, and some domestic plants. www.jlbryanbooks.com

Amanda Hocking lives in Minnesota and writes young adult paranormal romance and urban fantasy mostly. The *My Blood Approves* series is about vampires in Minneapolis. The Trylle Trilogy is a paranormal romance without vampires, shifters, mermaids, fae, angels, dragons, ghosts, or ninjas. Her latest books are *Hollowland*, a zombie urban fantasy set in the dystopian near future, and the novella *Letters to Elise*. *Honalee,* the first novel in her new Witches of Honalee series, will be available in 2011. http://amandahocking.blogspot.com/